CAGED ANIMAL

A NOAH WOLF THRILLER

DAVID ARCHER

RIGHTHOUSE

ISBN-13: 978-1-63696-115-6

ISBN-10: 1-63696-115-0

Cover design by: Damonza

Printed in the United States of America

www.righthouse.com

www.instagram.com/righthousebooks

www.facebook.com/righthousebooks

twitter.com/righthousebooks

NOAH WOLF THRILLERS

PROLOGUE

ALLISON LOOKED UP AS NOAH ENTERED HER OFFICE, but this time there was no smile waiting for him. She motioned for him to take the seat on the other side of her desk and waited until he had done so.

"I'm afraid I'm about to send you on a mission I don't want to give you," she said. "The CIA has specifically requested your assistance for one of their operatives." She let out a sigh. "Noah, you once knew an army captain by the name of Derek Simpson. Do you remember him?"

"Yes, of course," Noah said. "Captain Simpson was the prosecutor at my court-martial."

Allison nodded. "Yes, he was. Not long after that, he was recruited by the CIA and accepted. Since then, he has proven quite adept at recruiting assets of his own, particularly foreign nationals who are willing to share information with him. This mission will take you into Germany, where you will assist CIA Officer Derek Simpson with a new asset. Your particular job is going to be to make sure no one gets to him or the asset, to keep them safe; if it becomes known that you are American agents in the country, it could spark an international incident that might honestly lead to a new global war."

"All right," Noah said. "I notice that you are briefing me alone this time. What about my team?"

She shook her head. "That's why I hate sending you on this mission," Allison said. "They only want you, Noah. Your team is not going with you."

Noah nodded. "Is Simpson aware of who I am? That I was the sergeant he prosecuted for murders I didn't commit?"

Allison hesitated for only a second. "Unfortunately, you have to assume that he does. The CIA was deeply involved in tracking Monica Lord, I'm sure you remember that. She was able to get into your actual personnel files, and it's likely that she shared it with some of her CIA contacts. Considering his connection to your case, it's likely that someone privy to the information might have shared it with him."

"All right," Noah said. "I have no animosity toward him, of course, but I can't help wondering if he might have reservations about using me."

"Apparently not," Allison said. "According to the interagency request, he asked for you personally." She shrugged. "That could be based on your reputation, of course. You're considered our top agent in every way, and you already survived a number of situations that should have gotten you killed. If I were him and wanted the best, I would ask for you as well."

"That's understandable," Noah said. "When do I leave?"

She let out a sigh. "This afternoon," she said. She reached into a desk drawer and produced an envelope, which she passed to him. "Mission IDs and dossier packet. Your plane will be waiting at the airfield at two o'clock this afternoon. Weapons will be available when you get there, so there's no need to take anything with you." She looked him in the eye. "Noah—be careful. I want you coming back."

The rest of the day went by like a blur. Noah explained to Sarah, Neil, Marco and everyone else what was happening, then had to hurry to catch the plane that would take him to Nuremberg. It all happened so fast that they were all in shock, but Noah simply took it in stride.

For the duration of the mission, which was supposed to last two weeks, they would be cut off from any contact with Noah, and the thought just about drove Sarah crazy. As she kissed him goodbye, she made him promise once again to come home safely. "I don't know what I would do if I lost you," she said. "Especially now…"

"I'll be back," Noah said. He pulled her close and held her for another moment, then whispered in her ear. "I will always come back."

A moment later, he walked out the door and was gone. The longest two weeks of her life were about to begin.

The rest of the team stayed close to her after he left, each of them spending as much time with her as they could, but the best they could hope for was to keep her busy. Jenny and Neil spent most of the day with her, with Marco and Renée coming over in the evenings. Sometimes they all got together, going out to dinner or just hanging out at the house. They played cards, Monopoly and just about anything else they could think of to try to keep their minds off of what might be happening to Noah.

"The worst part," Sarah said after Monopoly one evening, "is waiting for the call that says something's gone wrong. We've had so many things go wrong on missions, I just—I'm just terrified of what could happen when I'm not with him."

Jenny looked at her and raised an eyebrow. "You're not going to be with him on missions much anymore," she said. "Soon as Allison finds out, she's going to bench you completely."

Sarah glanced down at her belly and rubbed her hand over it. "I'm not showing yet," she said. "Maybe I…"

Her phone rang. She looked at it for a moment, a brief look of terror on her face as she recognized Allison's name on the caller ID. She hit the speaker button as she answered, so that everyone could hear.

"Hello?"

"Sarah? It's Allison. I'm afraid I'm calling with some disturbing news."

Sarah's eyes went wide. "No," she said. "Allison, no..."

Jenny and Renée leaned close, both of them watching Sarah's face, while Neil and Marco stopped talking across the room and stared at the three women.

"Noah has been captured," Allison said. "As far as I know right now, he's alive, but he is in hostile hands. I got a call in to State already, and I'm going to do everything possible to get him back. I just thought you needed to be aware of what's happening."

"Where is he?" Marco demanded. "You've got to get us on the way, let us go in after him."

"Marco, that is impossible. As I said, I'm waiting for a return call from the State Department. We have forces not far away, and I'm hoping to get a SEAL team on this right away. If there's anything you can do, I promise I will call. In the meantime, I simply wanted Sarah to be aware of the situation. Sarah, please don't panic. I promise you I'm going to do everything possible to bring him back."

The line went dead, as it always did when Allison was finished talking. Sarah stared at the phone for a moment, then turned to her friends.

"He'll be back," she said. "He promised me. He promised me that he will always come back to me."

"Of course he will," Jenny said. "He may be a robot to some people, but that man loves you. He'll be back, I know he will."

Marco shook his head and ran his hands through his hair. "He'd be back a lot sooner if Allison would let us go," he said. "Well, if I knew where he was, I'd go on my own."

"He's at least halfway around the world from us, Marco," Neil said. "No matter what we did, we would probably be too late to do any good."

"It would be better than sitting here, waiting for another call."

They all turned to look at Sarah, but she was leaning back against the sofa. Her eyes were wide and staring straight ahead.

"Neil is right," she said softly. "There's really nothing we can do. We just have to trust that Allison can get him out of this. That's all we can do."

They all sat there together until the next morning. None of the others was willing to leave Sarah alone until the sun came up over the hills.

ONE

FIVE DAYS EARLIER

SOMEWHERE HIGH IN THE MOUNTAINS OF THE Bavarian Alps, Noah Wolf was on the run for his life. Tree branches were ripping at his clothes and scraping against his skin as he tripped and slipped on the muddy, uneven ground. His hands were scratched and bleeding, the wounds coated with a mixture of mud and slime from finding holds on trees, rocks and brush as he fought hard to stay upright.

The staccato sound of automatic weapons fire was echoing all around him, along with the angry voices of the men who were pursuing him. The sounds echoing among the trees and off the walls of the valley made it almost impossible to tell which direction they were coming from. When a branch near his face exploded in a shower of splinters, the only thing he could do was struggle to run faster and pray for a miracle.

He almost fell when, several yards ahead, the back of Derek Simpson's jacket suddenly erupted in a spray of blood and the big man's body collapsed, falling to the ground. Leaving a fallen comrade went against the very core of Noah's beliefs, but he couldn't stop. His gun was empty and his pursuers were right on his heels; to stop would mean certain and immediate death.

Just when he thought he couldn't continue, he caught a break in the form of a thick fog making its way through the valley, winding its way through the trees. He knew that if he could make it into that swirling mist, he would have at least a chance of escape, and it gave him the strength to carry on.

Ignoring the hail of bullets that was flying past him every second, Noah concentrated intently on putting one foot in front of the other. He would use the fog to lose his pursuers, and then circle back to find Derek. If the man was alive, they would find a way off the mountain and back to civilization. He pushed himself harder, his eyes firmly fixed on where he wanted to go.

He never felt the impact on the back of his skull as the bullet grazed him.

———

HE WOKE WITH A START, arms and legs reaching out and running into the walls of wherever he had awakened. Struggling for breath, the overwhelming odor that attacked his senses made him cough and gag. Scrambling into a sitting position, he found himself confused and disoriented.

He seemed to be in total darkness, and for a moment, he wondered if something had happened to his eyes, leaving him blind. The air was cold and damp, and the horrible smell was almost unbearable, but he simply ignored it. He lifted his hands up off the floor and looked at them, finding them coated in some sort of slimy sludge made up of mud and rotting vegetation.

He was in the bottom of a pit of some sort, he realized. As he felt around, he found that the floor was covered with rotten waste and the walls were slippery, as if they were made of thick clay mud. Cautiously he got to his feet, leaning against the slick, wet walls, his feet unsteady on the mounded garbage beneath them.

He stared upwards, hoping to see some sliver of light, but there was nothing.

Questions raced through his mind. Had he been buried alive? Had he been thrown into a pit to die alone and forgotten? Struggling, he clawed at the walls, his fingers digging into the mud as he desperately tried to climb out, but then he lost his grip and fell back. Knowing that he needed to rest before trying again, sitting on the floor, he leaned his head on his arms.

Considering what they had done, maybe this was what he deserved. He should have at least tried to stop Derek instead of just standing by.

His breath rattled in his throat as he forced himself to take stock of his circumstances. Only keeping his wits about him was going to get him out of this situation. Derek was almost certainly dead, and nobody had known where they were going after they left Germany. Derek had said they needed to tie up the loose ends from their mission, and that had brought them to this godforsaken part of the world.

He was on his own; if he was going to survive, he would have to figure out how to save himself. Getting to his feet again, he felt his way around the small prison. It was round, probably not much over six feet in diameter. Standing in the middle, he could stretch both arms out, barely touching the walls on either side.

A wave of dizziness put him back on the floor of the pit, reminding him that if he was going to survive, he would have to consider and address his injuries. Carefully, he felt his head. The back was covered in dried blood, and in the middle was a deep gouge that was still oozing more. Obviously, he had taken some sort of blow to the head, bad enough to split the skin and apparently knock him out. His entire body seemed to be rather badly bruised, as well, so his captors must have kicked or beaten him before dropping him into the hole. He sat there in the dark, trying to figure out a way to escape.

When you are faced with an insurmountable situation, it's necessary to introduce a variable into the equation. If he could get someone to acknowledge his presence, that might be a usable variable.

"Hey!" he shouted, but his voice barely made any noise at all, more like the croak of a frog than the shout of a man. He coughed and tried once more, hoping to catch the attention of anyone walking or standing nearby.

"Hello? Can somebody help me? I don't know why I'm here, I haven't done anything wrong." He listened for a moment, but there was no response; the only sound was a faint rustling noise coming from down near his feet. That was when he realized that he wasn't alone in his new environment. His cellmates in this prison were rats and insects, and they were foraging through the rubbish for food.

Hours passed, and Noah lost track of time. He was unable to rest because of the rats, who would climb all over him if he dared to sit down. He was hungry and thirsty, and growing weaker by the hour. He kept calling out in his passable German, doing what he could to maintain his cover. He just needed to explain to someone that it was all a big mistake, he had simply been in the wrong place at the wrong time, and if somebody would just come and talk to him, they could get it straightened out pretty quickly. He was only a businessman from Nuremberg whose car had broken down on the road. Eventually, though, his voice gave out, and eventually so did his legs and he ended up collapsing into the garbage.

He leaned against the wall with his arms wrapped around his body. He was sweating and shaking, feverish from whatever infection was probably taking root on the back of his head. Derek's face danced in front of his eyes. "Daniel betrayed us. We've got to clean up this mess as quickly and quietly as possible. He lives out in the countryside, near Bamberg. If we go now, we can be back in time for dinner." Daniel Reitner was a minor official in the German government; the traitorous double agent had lied about his ability to get them the information they had been sent to gather, creating a multitude of problems.

"Wake up! *Achtung*! Wake up!" Noah's eyes fluttered open at the sound of the strong German dialect. Above him, a long way up, he saw a narrow beam of light. He watched as a bottle was lowered down on a piece of string. "Water," the voice from above told him.

With fumbling fingers, he ripped the bottle from the string and drank down the delicious liquid inside. Before he could ask questions or say anything else, however, he was back in total darkness and alone once more. Gasping and choking because he drank too fast, he rested his back against the mud wall. His logical mind registered a single thought: if he was being given water, then they didn't want him dead.

At least, they didn't want him dead just yet.

Remaining conscious, however, proved to be difficult. He barely even noticed when a rat ran across his leg.

It had been Daniel Reitner, his elderly mother, his wife and two children, a housekeeper, a gardener and their families. All together, thirteen men, women and children, whom he had helped to round up, and then Derek had killed them all. What had he been thinking? Noah had walked away to stand guard, leaving Derek alone with the captives. He had known what was going to happen; down deep inside himself, he had known, but he hadn't stopped it.

The scene that greeted him when Derek called him back to help dispose of the bodies had looked like a slaughterhouse, yet he had helped pile them up in the kitchen, following Derek's orders blindly. A part of him simply wanted to walk away; instead, following orders, he set the charges that would turn the house into an inferno and hide what had happened.

The next time he woke up, he feebly kicked out at a rat gnawing on what remained of his right boot and shook his head, swiping at the flies and other bugs which were attracted to the blood still coating his head injury. He knew he was getting weaker all the time, and that he needed to make an attempt to get out before he was too weak to even care.

Caring; that made him think of Sarah. He thought of the promise he had made, to come back to her, and reached down inside himself for the strength to try again.

Struggling back to his feet, he tried to dig handholds in the walls, something to help him climb up out of the pit. It was slow going, and his fingers ached as he dug them into the hard packed mud. He managed to make it almost ten feet up the wall when he lost his grip and fell back, banging his head against the side and sinking once more into darkness.

His eyes opened, but he was too weak to move. His body had curled into the fetal position and his limbs felt heavy and numb. He considered the fact that he was going to die lying in rotten food waste, eaten alive by the creatures sharing his prison; he could feel bites on his legs even then. His eyes began to close; there was nothing to see anyway.

Sometime later, a noise disturbed him, cracks and bangs, followed by shouting in German and Russian, and then after a few minutes of silence, another voice speaking English with a brash American accent.

Noah made an effort to sit up, but it was too much. Light flooded into his tomb from above, causing him to bury his head in his hands; his eyes were too sensitive to bear the bright flashlight that was shining down onto him.

"Hey! Noah!"

He heard the words, but they made no sense, so he still didn't move. He had already realized that he was hallucinating at times, and his mind rejected the reality of what was happening. The welcoming sound of an American accent seemed so far out of place in this particular Hell that he figured he had to be imagining it.

"Hey, man! C'mon, grab the rope. We'll get you out." This was a second voice.

He ignored the rope that dangled in front of his eyes. It wasn't real, he knew, and nobody was coming to rescue him.

"Damn it," said the exasperated voice. "Belay that line, I'll have to climb down and get him."

Noah barely felt rope being tied around his body, or being lifted up into the fresh air. He lay limp, unresponsive to the voices and the touch of hands tending to his injuries. The only indication he gave that he was alive were four words mumbled in German.

"*Ich habe nichts getan*," he said.

"What was that?" It was the first voice he had heard, but it was the second voice that replied.

"He said, 'I didn't do anything.'"

Noah looked up, barely able to open his eyes to focus on the man in the blacked out, special forces gear. The soldier looked back at him, and then shook his head. "Don't worry, kid," he said. "We're the good guys."

TWO

LIEUTENANT COMMANDER JAMES LARSEN SAT ON A folding chair in his commanding officer's temporary command center at the Sigonella Naval Base in Italy, on the island of Sicily. He had arrived with his team less than half an hour earlier and had barely been given time to get his kit off the plane before being called in to the briefing.

From overhead came the faint whir of a ceiling fan turning slowly, circulating the hot, dry air that filled the makeshift office. Larsen listened to his CO's voice as he studied the contents of the file he had just been handed: reconnaissance photographs, weather reports, thermal images of troop movements in the target area; all the standard information necessary for a mission in a hostile environment.

"This is a rush job. It just came in from the State Department last night," his CO explained. "Two days ago, a missing CIA agent turned up at a rural medical clinic outside Nuremberg. He had been shot up pretty badly, two holes in his back. It took them until last night to confirm his identity."

"If they have their agent, what do they want with us?" Larsen asked as he turned to another page, and a name jumped out at him. "Derek Simpson. Are we talking about *the* Derek Simpson?"

He growled the question as he read the name of the injured agent.

"The same. Didn't you work with him last year? Where was it, Afghanistan?"

"Yeah. Extracting a particularly nasty ISIS leader." Working with Simpson wasn't an experience he wanted to repeat. He turned back to the file and began to study the mission. "This says Crimean soldiers are rumored to have captured an American spy in country, somebody they're accusing of assassinating the family of one of their government officials. That sounds like a job Derek would relish, but if he escaped..." Larsen kept the rest of his thought to himself.

"Langley thinks they're talking about Noah Wolf," his commanding officer filled in the gap, "from E & E. Apparently he was assigned as backup for Simpson on his most recent mission."

Larsen looked up at his commander, surprise registering on his face. "*Camelot*?" Larsen raised an eyebrow. He hadn't had a lot of direct dealings with E & E, but he knew who they were. The only things he really knew about Camelot personally, however, were the many legends surrounding the assassin.

"I believe that's what they call him in intelligence circles. He was in Germany with Simpson, they were there acquiring details on the status of the German deal with the Russians, but apparently something went wrong. The Russians are operating out of Crimea, which is why Crimean soldiers are involved. The asset is presumed dead after his house went up in flames five nights ago, and Noah and Simpson went MIA about the same time. At least, that's what everyone thought until Simpson turned up half dead two days ago. According to the chatter, Noah was captured in Germany and then transported by helicopter to an operational base in Ukraine."

"So Camelot is the Crimeans' American spy? Is his boss losing her mind yet?"

"That's putting it mildly, she's been screaming at State ever since she got the word. Simpson's no help, the man's been unconscious since he staggered into the med center. I need you to go in and get him out before they parade him on TV and questions start getting asked at the UN and NATO."

Larsen closed the file. The soldiers making the claims were located in a hotly disputed area of Ukraine, a section that was seeing a lot of action between local militia and Russian forces. It wasn't going to be an easy extraction. "So what's the plan? A full team is going to be hard to get in and out unseen. Didn't the militia in that area shoot down a Russian helicopter last week?"

His commander nodded, his expression grim. "We know for sure that they've got surface to air missiles, probably mortars and even nastier stuff. I'm sending in you and the new guy, Barron, to locate Camelot and assess the situation. If the mission is a go, I'll send in the rest of the team as support. Once the support team is on the ground, you and Barron will extract Noah, and here's the tricky part." He paused. "The nearest extraction point is twelve miles away from Camelot's last known location."

"We have to carry an injured man out twelve miles?" Larsen asked. "Through hostile territory?"

His CO nodded. "I know it's going to be tough. The whole area is in an uproar, but that's the nearest safe place to land a helicopter. You'll be dodging both Crimean and Ukrainian forces, and possibly even Russian military forces, all the way out." He paused again this time, though his expression changed to one of distaste. "So with that in mind, if you think this guy is too badly injured to move or you can't reach him, order Barron to set the laser targeting system and we'll send in a drone."

Larsen pursed his lips, unhappy with this final order, but after a moment, he nodded. It was a sad fact of life on the SEAL team that you couldn't always save the day. If they couldn't get Camelot out safely, they were to eliminate him and leave no trace whatsoever of his existence. If there was no captured spy, there could be no embarrassing questions at the UN or in Congress.

———

THE REAR of the military cargo plane was empty except for the two men who sat opposite each other, carefully checking over all of their equipment. Larsen finished tightening the straps that crossed his chest, making sure his parachute was firmly in place for the HALO jump he was about to make. Glancing up, he studied his teammate, the new guy in his SEAL team, Barron Barron.

"How many jumps have you made, Barron?" Larsen shouted over the noise of the aircraft.

Barron looked up from where he was doing his own checks. "I stopped counting after the first hundred and fifty. I love this shit, man," he shouted back. "I got into base jumping on my last leave, and then I had to try out the new wing suits." He grinned as he tightened up his harness and picked up his rifle. "Feels like flying, almost makes you feel like you might be Superman. I tell you, I love this job. Jumping outta planes and shooting stuff up? There ain't nothing better."

Shooting stuff up! Larsen shook his head and got to his feet. Dealing with a youngster like Barron made him feel old. He tried to remember when he had last felt so much enthusiasm. In his mid thirties now, he woke up every day with aches and pains from years of putting his body through abuse. He trained every day and ate properly to keep up with men who were often as much as ten years younger than himself.

The jump master came down to where they stood, running his own check over their jump equipment, cueing them to attach their oxygen masks before opening the doors. As the cold air hit him in the face, Larsen couldn't help the grin that spread across his face. Who was he kidding? He was thirty-six years old and he was about to jump out of a plane and 'shoot stuff up' in an attempt to rescue an injured man.

The funny thing was, he couldn't think of a single thing he would rather be doing.

Larsen and Barron left the plane at fourteen thousand feet, free falling for just over a minute before opening their chutes at three thousand feet above ground level. They came in silently and undetected five miles away from the spot where it was believed Noah was being held prisoner. Larsen guided them in with the GPS attached to his wrist.

On the ground, they quickly stripped their harnesses and gathered the parachutes, hiding the evidence of their arrival under nearby bushes. Without taking a break, Larsen led the way toward the coordinates he had been provided. Moving quickly and quietly down the mountainside, Larsen set as fast a pace as he felt was safe. The satellite photos they had studied had helped them plan a route down the mountain that would hopefully let them avoid contact with any of the forces between them and their goal.

As they neared the coordinates, they slowed, creeping forward when they heard the soft crackle of a camp fire and the faint murmur of male voices. Larsen pointed out a small knoll over-looking the camp. Crawling on their bellies, knives in hand, the two men slipped past a dozing sentry to reach Larsen's designated sniper perch.

Lying flat, both men looked down at the camp below. With Barron serving as spotter, watching for anybody trying to sneak up on their position, Larsen fitted a thermal imaging scope to his rifle and scanned the area. It took him a little while to work out the layout of the camp and get a head count of the soldiers they would have to deal with.

"I think I've found him," he said. "If I'm right, he's in a hole in the ground, and looks to be in a bad way." Larsen spoke softly, keeping his eye on the unmoving figure, whose shape and body heat seemed to be mixed with whatever he was laying on.

After a moment, Larsen shifted back and handed Barron the rifle. "How many men do you see down there?" Larsen asked. He had done his own count, but wanted confirmation.

"Forty-five, maybe five more with the sentries." That matched with Larsen's own count, and he went back to watching the camp through the scope.

Sucking in his cheeks, Larsen knew that if he was following his orders to the letter, the fact that whoever was in that pit was barely alive and guarded by fifty armed men was plenty of reason to tell Barron to fix the targeting laser and consign Noah to his fate. The trouble was, Larsen hated the idea of leaving a fallen man to die, sacrificed to protect a bunch of politicians from having to own up to the truth. He took a pair of binoculars and studied the surrounding terrain. He had an idea of how he could pull off an extraction, and if it worked, they would get away safely and have a good story to tell when it was over. If it went wrong, they would all be dead and none of them would care if a few politicians got raked over the coals.

"Keep watch. I'm making the call," Larsen ordered, his mind made up. "We'll go for the extraction tonight. Meanwhile, we need to set up some sort of a diversion so we can clear the camp. With everybody off chasing their tails in the dark, we can slip in and get him out without anybody being the wiser."

"Awesome," Barron said with a grin. He had just made a night time high altitude jump and now he was getting to play with explosives. While he was watching the camp, he had spotted a man with the Russian version of a bazooka. With a bit of luck, that particular weapon would be in his hands before the night was over.

While Larsen made the call to send in the rest of his team, Barron kept his eyes trained on the camp. Afterward, Larsen took over surveillance, his attention focused on the young assassin in the pit, whose body had moved just enough to convince Larsen that he had made the right decision. Barron began preparing the explosive charges they would use to create a diversion.

At eighteen hundred hours, Larsen received word that the rest of his team was on the way, ETA twenty two hundred. The sky was getting darker. Most of the soldiers in the camp were sitting around the three small camp fires, eating some form of field ration. In the hours they had been watching the camp, Larsen noticed that nobody had approached the pit holding the prisoner.

"Okay," he said, "let's get this show on the road." Larsen crawled backward until he was clear of the knoll.

Barron's white teeth almost seemed to glow against the dark of his camo face paint as a grin split his face. Moving apart, they approached the camp from different sides, silently eliminating the sentries guarding the camp and planting their distractions on the way to their planned positions. When the support team was on the ground and ready, both men were in place. Each activated his detonator, setting off the first round of charges.

The resulting explosions sent up clouds of earth and tree roots and the noise reverberated off the valley walls. To add to the confusion, Larsen and Barron fired their rifles into the camp. As the soldiers came running out, they moved in silently, quickly eliminating the last few left to stand guard.

Barron pulled the heavy wooden cover off the pit holding the prisoner. "Hey! Noah!" he called out, shining a flashlight into the hole.

The man lying there moved to block the light, but didn't respond. Barron dropped a line into the hole toward him.

"Hey, man! C'mon, grab the rope. We'll get you out." Larsen stepped up beside Barron and looked into the hole, his eyes watering at the stench. He gritted his teeth when Noah flinched away from the rope.

"Damn it. Belay that line, I'll have to climb down and get him." He waited for Barron to snub the line around a tree.

Trying his best not to breathe more than necessary, Larsen lifted the limp body and looped the rope around his chest. Once he had Noah secured, he climbed out and then the two of them pulled the injured assassin up out of the pit.

James Larsen looked at the filthy, bloody body laying before him. Under the dim firelight, Camelot looked as if he was dying, with a massive laceration to the back of his skull that was obviously infected.

"Sir, we need to get moving before they regroup. Is he ready to move?" Barron was keeping watch as Larsen made his assessment. The last of their explosives had gone off and the soldiers would be returning at any moment.

"He will be soon," Larsen replied. Cleaning Noah's arm as best he could, he put in an IV, sending fluids, antibiotics and painkillers into his patient's body. He found a tarpaulin and placed Noah onto it, and then the two of them carried the limp body between them, leaving as fast as they could.

They kept moving, dodging the patrols that were searching for them. At one point, Larsen ordered a stop and called for a Med-Evac, but the area they were in was too dangerous and he was told it wasn't going to be possible. His original orders would still apply, to join the rest of his team and carry Noah out through twelve miles of hostile territory to a safe zone.

"No evac," Larsen said. "Our original orders stand." He looked at his maps, then pointed ahead. "There are some caves half a mile up, on that slope. We can lay low there while I try to get Noah stabilized enough for the rest of the hike."

By midnight, they were hiding in one of the many caves that peppered the mountainside. Noah lay shivering but cleaned up, dressed loosely in Larsen's spare BDU. Larsen was changing the IV bag, but he was concerned about the shape Noah was in.

"I didn't do anything," Noah mumbled, not actually conscious. "Wasn't anything I could do. Derek, why did you do that?" He almost sounded like he was whining and he idly tried to pull the catheter out of his arm.

"No, you don't," Larsen said, catching his hand and pinning it down. For a moment, Noah struggled, but then felt back into a deep sleep.

Larsen looked at the expression on Noah's face and wondered exactly what Derek had done.

THREE

Lieutenant Commander Larsen sat just inside the entrance to the cave, keeping watch on the valley that stretched out below him. In the darkness, the lights of their Crimean pursuers could be seen clearly, dancing beams of light that flickered between the tall trees. An occasional shout rang out as their pursuers found clues to the direction they had taken.

Larsen shifted uneasily. He could hear the search party getting closer. It had been almost impossible to hide their trail, two men carrying a third on a makeshift tarpaulin stretcher while holding weapons. It had been all they could do to stay ahead of the searchers.

He glanced back into the cave, noting Barron's sleeping form sitting against the cave wall. Larsen had told him to rest while they waited for the remainder of the team.

From another part of the cave, barely visible in the dim light of the green glow sticks, he heard the raspy voice of the rescued spy.

"I should have done something. Should have stopped you, I should have."

With a sigh, Larsen got wearily to his feet. At least Noah was speaking English now, but it meant he was making noise. When he got to the the makeshift stretcher, where Noah was wrapped in both his and Barron's blankets, Larsen put a hand on his shoulder.

"Hey, Noah," he said, "you've got to be quiet." Larsen kept his voice low, barely above a whisper.

"Derek?" Noah asked weakly.

"No, I'm Lieutenant Commander James Larsen. Derek isn't here."

Any hope that Noah was coming out of his delirium was squashed as the injured spy's eyes closed again and he went back to mumbling in a mixture of English, German and Russian.

Sitting back on his heels, Larsen took a moment to think about what he was hearing. The parts he could understand made his blood run cold. He knew the sort of operations Simpson liked to sign on for. The man was well known and famously ruthless, but Larsen could see clearly the effect that working alongside Derek was having on Noah.

Just before the Kabul assignment, Larsen had learned through one of his many contacts in the intelligence community the reason why they called Noah Wolf "Camelot." He was E & E's apparently unbeatable assassin; he and his team got to take on all the dirty jobs. The trouble was that Noah Wolf wasn't a psychopath. He was a cold, logical and very efficient killer, but he also had a strong sense of what was right and what was wrong. A man like Derek knew the difference, but didn't give a damn.

"I didn't do anything," Noah muttered. "I wasn't even there when it happened…" He was talking again.

"Hey. Shh, quiet," Larsen urged, tucking the blankets tighter around Noah's body before moving back to the cave entrance to check on the position of the rapidly approaching enemy.

———

I DIDN'T DO ANYTHING. Nothing. I should have stopped you. Why did you do it, Derek?

There was blood pooling around the bodies; the floor in the corner of the large kitchen was slippery with it. The dead, accusing eyes of a child had been staring up at him, looking straight into his soul.

How could I have let this happen? I could have stopped him. I knew what he was going to do, it was obvious.

"What, kid?" Derek had said when it was over. "They call it 'wet work' for a reason, you know." Derek smiled as he let Reitner's body tumble to the floor.

This isn't right, he thought. *He shouldn't have done this.*

He reached under his left arm for his pistol.

Derek's eyes were locked onto him, the excitement of the kill making them seem to glow. He smiled, the delighted smile of a true psychopath.

"Go for it, kid." The smile on Derek's face urged Noah to close his hand around the grip and draw the weapon. What Derek had done was far beyond the mission they were given, and could conceivably start a war. This was the same man who had once prosecuted him for taking action against his own squad mates, against his superior officer; now he had done something as horrible as the act that had prompted Noah's actions then.

"Well," Derek asked. "Got anything to say?"

Noah stared at him, and for the first time in many years, he wasn't sure what to do. Everything inside him was saying that he should take Simpson out, eliminate him on the spot and report back about what had happened, but he was only the man's cover on this mission. He wasn't the one in charge, and that left him uncertain. It wasn't a feeling he was familiar with.

"It's the job," Derek said. "Kill or be killed. If you were in my position, you would have killed them all yourself. I just saved you the trouble."

I didn't do anything.

"Oh come on, kid, since when did you become so high and mighty? You're Camelot, you've got plenty of blood on your hands."

The words echoed through his mind again as he lay there, feverish dreams making the whole situation seem even more dire than it had been.

"They call it wet work for a reason."

―――――

"Hey, Noah, you've gotta be quiet."

"Derek?" Derek was there? No, wait, Derek was dead.

"No. It's James Larsen. Navy SEALs, they sent us in to bring you home." James Larsen? Noah didn't recognize the name.

Deep breaths. He made himself take deep breaths and forced himself to concentrate, but it was hard to focus on what was real and what was still part of the dream. His mind took him back, told him to pull himself together. All he had to do was follow Simpson's orders, set the damned charges and get out of there. It was far too late to do anything else, he knew, but he could report to Allison when he got back. That was the only option left to him at that point. Survive, and report what Simpson had done.

"I didn't do anything." How many times had he heard that same excuse from others, and known that they were only lying to themselves? His eyes closed once again.

The last of the charges was set, and all he had to do was press the button on the detonator. It would all go up, and they could leave, head for extraction and back to safety. Noah could make his report and let it go, put it behind him. Another mission would come, and then he could focus on that one.

I wasn't even there.

―――――

"Hey. Shhh, quiet." Larsen's voice brought him back out of the recurring nightmare again, and he clung to it like a lifeline. He could feel the cool, fresh air, the rough blanket wrapped around him, all the signs that he had been pulled out of hell. He lifted his hands and looked at them, turning them slowly before his eyes.

Even though it wasn't there anymore, he could still see the blood of innocents. Noah had always done his best to avoid taking an innocent life, but Derek Simpson didn't have any such compunctions.

He could still hear the muffled sobs of the frightened children coming from inside the farmhouse, the voices of the women begging Daniel Reitner to tell these madmen what they wanted to know. He heard the soft noise of Derek's silenced Beretta, and the sickening thud of another body hitting the floor as the others screamed and cried.

He had gone back inside, but he stopped in the kitchen and stared down at the broken bodies and the dull, lifeless eyes of the victims. He handed Derek the detonator. "You do it," he said without any trace of emotion. "Let's get this over with."

"Oh, cheer up, kid. I'll buy dinner when we get back to the hotel. Maybe those pretty little waitresses will be on duty in the restaurant, and we can get lucky. Take your mind off of things, right?"

The farmhouse disintegrated in a fireball, the obvious evidence of their presence gone in less than a second. "Good job, kid," Derek said. "Good job."

It was over, for the moment. All they had to do was get back to the hotel and then wait for extraction. He was almost finished with Derek Simpson, and it couldn't come too soon.

"You're safe. Another hour and our ride will be here, and we'll get you back home." The stranger's voice woke him from his nightmare.

"Home?" Noah asked. Running his tongue over his lips, he felt cracked, tender skin. In the dim light of a couple of glow sticks, he vaguely recognized the man watching over him as a friend.

"Yeah, home, kid," Larsen smiled. This was better.

"Don't call me that," Noah said calmly. "Don't call me kid."

"Okay, how about Camelot, or do you prefer Noah?" He was pretty sure he could wipe brain damage off the list of Noah's complications. Now if the whites of Noah's eyes would just lose the faint yellowing, he would be able to remove liver damage from the list as well.

"Noah's fine."

Tiredness was pulling him back under. He didn't want to go. He could already see tiny hands holding a teddy bear waiting for him in the darkness.

———

"How's he doin', sir?"

Larsen turned to look up at his subordinate. "A bit better. You're supposed to be catching up on your sleep."

"I'm fine, sir, ready to go."

Larsen looked at his watch. It was nearly time to make a move anyway. "Okay, let's get ready to move out."

He got to his feet and went to look over the valley below. The lights had vanished; the area had grown quiet. Larsen's eyes followed the soundless flight of an owl circling above the trees, scanning for prey that was scurrying about in the undergrowth far below. Suddenly, it dropped from the sky, zeroing in on its next meal, a sure sign that there were no soldiers lying in wait.

He had ordered his support team to draw the search parties away, and it looked like the strategy had been successful. It was safe now for them to leave the cave and make their way toward the extraction point more than a dozen miles away. The support team would rendezvous with them shortly after daylight, and from then on, it would be a hard slog to safety. If all went well, he figured they could be back at the base within forty-eight hours.

———

Sigonella Naval Base, Italy.

Derek Simpson woke up in a hospital bed. Although he was instantly alert, he pretended to be unconscious while he worked out what was happening around him. He watched through barely-open eyes as a nurse attached a variety of monitoring sensors to his arms and chest. The throb from his shoulder wound told him they had already examined that injury, and the feeling of a dressing being firmly placed over his left hip told him a second person was in the room.

He had obviously slept through the transfer from the medical facility. The local doctors had been easy to fool; acting dazed and confused had gotten him two days of much needed rest. Then, once they had treated his wounds, he had told them his name and who to contact. Now that he was back, however, he was going to have to figure out how to explain the blown mission and how his partner had died, his body left in enemy hands.

He kept up the ruse until he was alone, with only the steady beeping of the heart monitor for company. He closed his eyes again and went over the final hours of the mission in his memory, trying to figure out where things had actually gone wrong.

The chill in the air, the fog that moved between the trees, and even the dampness in the air had all added to the anticipation of the kill. They were predators on the hunt, top of the food chain, and nobody was going to stand in their way.

Having lured the first of the weary guards into an ambush, Derek stood back to watch Noah go to work. He grinned coldly at the way the young assassin took him down. It was a classic Noah Wolf move: quick and without hesitation. The snapping of the guard's neck had sounded like the crack of a twig under a boot. It had actually helped to draw the second guard over to their position.

Ah, and then the second man had warmed his heart. Noah had stepped from the shadows and strangled him with his bare hands. It had reminded Derek of a younger version of himself. There was nothing like an up close kill, feeling the life leave the body of an enemy.

Noah was a natural, Derek thought. He was wasted with E&E.

"Who the hell authorized sedating Simpson? I need him up and answering questions." Derek was jerked awake by angry voices coming from outside his room. Allison Peterson? What the hell was she doing here? He raised his head slightly and saw the door to his room swinging shut. The bitch must have been standing right over him.

"The doctors in Germany had dosed him for transport, ma'am. I've already spoken to Captain Miller, he says Officer Simpson should wake up soon." That sounded like one of Peterson's own people, probably fresh out of college somewhere.

"Well, while we wait for Agent Simpson to join us, I want to find out exactly what happened in Germany. Get me every single scrap of intel we have on Daniel Reitner, and then light a fire under every intelligence source we have in the region."

"Yes, ma'am."

"It was supposed to be nothing but a damned intelligence gathering mission, and now we've got two agents down and a literally blown asset! Why are you still standing here? Go!"

Derek couldn't help the hint of a smile that curved his lips. Director Peterson was pissed.

"Ma'am—I—I already put the Reitner file on your desk, and I've requested the German source send a report in ASAP."

Derek sneered; he was right, a college kid. What was the government doing hiring damn glorified office clerks?

"Thank you, Michael," Peterson said, softening only slightly. It seemed the clerk had shut Peterson up for once—or maybe not. "Now, get me some information on what happened at the Reitner farm. I want to know how the hell this thing went south, and I want to know now! And make damn sure Captain Miller understands that I want to know as soon as Simpson is capable of answering questions, and then find out the ETA on Noah's arrival."

FOUR

So the bitch was here to speak to him. Well, E & E Director Allison Peterson would just have to wait until he was ready to speak to her. She might be his boss for the moment, but as far as he was concerned, that only meant it was her job to deal with the all the crap that got in the way of him getting back out into the field.

Lying back, he began his own mental debrief. As near as he could figure, it had been six days since the wild chase through the forest.

His lips curved up into a smile. "Noah's arrival," she had said. He had thought Noah was dead. It seemed like maybe Derek wasn't the only one who was hard to kill.

Blue eyes narrowed in concentration as Derek began to run through all the possible scenarios.

If Noah had been in the hands of the enemy all that time, was he in any sort of condition to give a report? He had heard the cries from their pursuers. They had been shouting about capturing one of the assassins. So, yes, Noah had been captured and Peterson obviously thought he was up to answering questions.

So that led to the next question.

If Noah was capable of talking, would he? No, Noah would keep quiet, just like he was doing.

Noah would keep his mouth shut while he worked out how much trouble he was in. Because as much as Noah might try to deny it, he might as well have been pulling the trigger himself. What happened in that house was a necessity, but the bleeding hearts in D.C. wouldn't see it that way.

Noah had handed him the detonator. "Let's get this over with," he'd said. He had almost been pouting, acting like a little bit of spilt blood was some sort of problem.

He had taken the detonator and pressed the button with his thumb; the farmhouse had disintegrated in a magnificent fireball, all of it gone in less than a second. In that moment, he had forgiven Noah for his attitude.

"Good job, kid," he had said. Nobody could say that Derek Simpson didn't give credit where it was due, but Noah had only looked at him without saying a word.

Staring up at the ceiling, Derek grinned, remembering the scene of destruction. He doubted there was one brick left on top of another. Noah was good with explosives. It was a skill Derek had never bothered with. He preferred his kills to be up close and personal, or, if that wasn't possible, from a distance with a sniper rifle or poison. Bombs were effective, but they made one hell of a mess. On the other hand, they also destroyed an awful lot of incriminating evidence.

He relaxed. That was it. All the evidence had been destroyed. The only ones who knew what happened was Noah and himself. He just had to decide on what that truth was and make sure Noah repeated it.

———

IN THE CRIMEAN FOREST, the morning sun was slowly rising higher in the sky, the warmth burning away the last of an early morning mist. Under the vast canopy overhead, sunlight was just breaking through between the branches to send out flickering shadows across the forest floor, helping to camouflage the eight men who were moving through the heavily wooded terrain. The only sound betraying their presence was made by the soft squelches of their booted feet as they traveled over the muddy ground. Suddenly, the man in the lead held up a fist and they all came to an immediate halt. As one, they all silently sank down to the ground.

Moving slowly, James Larsen crept forward to the lead man's side and followed the line of his arm to where he pointed out a man and a young boy walking along a forest trail. The man was carrying an ax and the boy was pulling a simple wooden sledge, presumably to drag the logs they were going to cut back to their home. The SEAL team waited in silence for the pair to pass by and then continued on, even more cautiously than before.

An hour later, Larsen called a halt, sending two men off to scout the route toward the extraction point and ordering the rest to spread out and keep watch while he checked on Noah. Crouching down beside Noah, Larsen set up fresh bags of IV fluids and antibiotics. Then he turned to the task of checking out the head wound. Removing the sticky, foul smelling dressing, he noticed fresh infection leaking from the swollen laceration. After cleaning out the pus, he dropped all the equipment he had used into a plastic bag and placed it all into his pack. As in any covert mission, they were leaving nothing of themselves behind.

As he finished off, he noticed Noah was watching him through pain-filled eyes. "Hey, Noah, how are you feeling?"

"Fine," the younger man mumbled, trying to look around, but stopping when the slight movement rubbed at the wound. "Where are we?" he asked.

"We're on our way out of Crimea. What do you remember?" Larsen asked, pleased to see that the fever had broken as the antibiotics worked their magic on the infection.

"I'm not sure, everything is kinda hazy," Noah replied, his eyes sliding shut before he forced them open again.

"Hazy, huh?" Larsen returned, his tone letting Noah know he wasn't fooled at all.

"Yeah, hazy," Noah agreed, his eyes sliding shut again.

Larsen sat back on his heels, a worried frown on his face. Noah's delirium-fueled confession had been playing on his mind ever since he had heard the first garbled plea of, "Why'd you do it, Derek?" There was no way that the younger man could have forgotten what had happened back in that farmhouse. Clearing his throat, Larsen gently touched Noah's shoulder.

"Listen, Noah, you should think about it. If Simpson did something he wasn't supposed to do..."

Noah's eyes snapped open, his expression stoic. "Nothing happened. I would have remembered. We didn't do anything." A little taken aback by the look in the younger man's eyes, Larsen dropped the subject. If Noah thought this matter would end out in the wilds of Crimea, he was going to be in for a nasty shock when he got back to the airbase.

"Why don't you try to get some more sleep?" Larsen suggested, doing his best to hide his disappointment at Noah's subterfuge.

———

"You've pulled a job with Derek Simpson? Well, good luck with that."

Larsen had looked at his buddy from Military Intelligence and frowned. "What's that supposed to mean?" he asked. "Hell, I know the guy is a ghoul. Everyone knows that."

"Ghoul? Ha! That's putting it mildly. Jeez, you should check out who you're working with, Larsen. The guy is notorious for getting people around him killed."

"I've worked with Simpson before," Larsen said. "I wouldn't want to do it again, but hey, orders are orders. Yeah, he's a loose cannon, but..." Privately, he had always considered Simpson to be more like a freelance psychopath, but there was no denying he got the

job done. It wasn't like Langley would want to hear his opinion, anyway.

"I mean it, Larsen. There's plenty of scuttlebutt floating around about Simpson... And you know about this Camelot character?"

"Noah Wolf? Yeah, I know who he is. Works for Peterson, out of Neverland." He had looked into the other man's eyes. "Why, what have you heard?"

"Sir? We're ready to move out."

Larsen pulled himself back to the present. He was getting tired. He looked up at Barron, who was watching him closely. Had the new man on the team noticed his inattention?

"Right." Larsen got to his feet and gestured for his team to move out. He watched as Barron and Pratt picked up the stretcher and the whole team began to move off.

"Well, let's just say Simpson's finally found a kindred spirit." Larsen took up a rearguard position. Was his buddy right? Was Noah really just Camelot, nothing more than a weapon at the disposal of his E & E masters?

———

DEREK WOKE up to the sound of a metal chair being dragged across the linoleum flooring. Moving carefully, he sat up, locking eyes with a nervous looking young man wearing brand new fatigues and the shiniest pair of laced boots he had ever seen. This, he guessed, was Peterson's aide. Michael looked even younger than he had expected.

The young man flushed under Derek's gaze, reminding the spy of a deer caught in the headlights. He did nothing to set the boy at ease, smirking when the younger man finally dropped his eyes to the floor and hurriedly finished setting up a metal table and a chair next to the bed. Satisfied that Peterson's college boy knew his place, Derek leaned back against his pillows and ignored the young man while he waited for Director Peterson to put in her inevitable appearance.

He had faced countless debriefs over the years, and in his opinion, nearly every one of them was a waste of time. All the Bureau Chiefs and politicians were interested in was the final results. Nobody actually wanted the full details of his assignments written down. Plausible deniability was a by-word for most of the jobs he was assigned to, so why was Peterson so eager to get his statement this time?

The aide suddenly jumped. Derek's attention snapped to the door as it swung open and E & E Director Allison Peterson walked into the room. Derek studied her appearance; she was dressed for working in the field. Her long, dark blonde hair hung down her back in a thick strand. Her fatigues, unlike her aide's, were faded and worn. He tried to think of the last time he had seen her in anything other than power suits and high heels.

"Agent Simpson." She spoke crisply, her blue eyes cool, calm and focused.

"Director Peterson. You shouldn't have bothered." He shot her a smile, baring his teeth in an insincere smile when he saw her brow crease in irritation.

Sitting down on the steel chair, she rested her arms on the table and leaned forward.

"This is just a preliminary debrief on your recent actions in Germany. Would you care to explain how a simple fishing expedition turned into such a colossal screw-up?" She returned his smile.

"Is he old enough to be listening to an adult conversation?" Derek hooked his chin toward Peterson's aide.

"Let's just get this over with, shall we?" she replied. Flipping open a notepad, she looked up at him, waiting for him to speak.

"A screw-up? That's a bit unfair, don't you think?" He crossed his arms over his chest, barely managing to hide how much the movement hurt his shoulder.

"Oh, I think I'm being quite fair with my assessment. The asset is dead and his home destroyed. Camelot was captured close to the scene and somehow identified as an American assassin. We have alienated some powerful allies and have given our adversaries ammunition to use against us. In what way would you define your assignment as a success?"

Oh, so she was going to play it like that, was she? Trying to pin the blame on good ol' Derek Simpson for her own mistake in sending that kid on this mission.

"It was the intelligence people who put us onto Reitner," Derek said, putting the blame firmly where he believed it belonged. "We followed established protocol and made contact. It was only because of my experience that I caught on that something was off with the asset, and it was my decision to bug his home and office. It was because of this I discovered he was in fact an FSB double agent."

"Are you telling me Reitner was employed by the Russians?" She raised an eyebrow.

"That's exactly what I'm telling you, lady. If it wasn't for me, Moscow would be able to listen in on everything we shared with our so-called allies in Germany, and probably anyone else in the EU. Reitner was a popular guy."

Derek watched as Peterson leaned back in her chair, her eyes fixed on his face, weighing the truth of his statement.

"So what made you so suspicious?" she asked.

"He was too eager to help," Derek replied. "When we went out to his home, I kept him talking while the ki—Noah bugged various parts of the house, including the phone. It was two days later we heard him talking on the phone, discussing turning two Americans over to his FSB handler."

"And why didn't you pass this intel back up the line?" Peterson demanded. "We could have turned Reitner, or used him to pass on disinformation."

"Because I knew you would require more proof than a recorded conversation, and I was certain I could turn the man a lot quicker than anybody else you've got working in the region." He paused, turning to lock his cold gaze on the director's aide. "I am very good at making people change their minds."

Michael cringed. Seeing the young man pale under his threatening gaze warmed Derek's heart.

"Leave him alone, Simpson," Peterson warned, but there was a slight smile on her lips. "So you planned to turn Reitner?"

"That was the idea. However, the man pulled a gun on us as soon as we arrived at his home."

"And neither you or Noah, two very experienced agents, could disarm him safely?" Disbelief was plain in her voice.

"He had his bodyguards behind us," Derek answered smoothly. "We were outnumbered."

"Let me get this straight. You're telling me two highly trained operatives, one of whom has been known to shoot his way out of a trap set by a full Spetsnaz team, let a lowly government official and two of his servants take them captive?"

"I wanted to bring Reitner in. Exposing him as a traitor would have helped your negotiations with the Germans, but the man was insane. We ended up having to fight our way out. We had only just reached our car when the whole damn house blew up. Reitner is the only one who could have done it."

Allison's eyes narrowed as she looked at him. "So, you're telling me Reitner killed himself and his family? Come on, Simpson."

Derek could tell she didn't believe him.

"He must have," he said, his face reflecting his sincerity. "Hey, we barely got out of there with our lives! The explosion brought soldiers down from the mountain and they took out our car. We had to make our escape on foot, through the forest."

"So what happened next? How did you get separated?"

"In the trees," he said smoothly. "They were coming at us from all angles. I was shot and went down, and I don't know what happened after that." He smiled at her, all teeth and a mocking light in his eyes. She had no choice but to take his word for it. Most of it was true anyway and, once Noah confirmed the story, Peterson would be forced to sit on her doubts.

Besides, it was her fault they were in the mess in the first place.

She was the one who had insisted on sending one of her people along. If she had let the CIA do their jobs without interference, this probably would never have happened.

That's what Langley would say, anyway.

"It's a nice story, Simpson," she said, "very nice. I don't suppose you have any kind of proof of any of this?"

His smile widened further. "Well yes, I do, darlin'. The recording should still be in the hotel room, under the baseboard, just under the window."

At the 'darlin'' comment, Peterson had gotten to her feet, the chair skidding back and toppling over. She leaned across the table, her professional demeanor wiped away by Derek's disrespect. "You may call me Director, Ma'am or even Sir, if you damn well like, Simpson. You use any other form of address again, I'll have you up on report so damn quick, it'll knock that smirk of yours to the other side of your face."

Derek hid his surprise at her outburst. Usually nothing he said or did flustered people like her.

He thought about it for a moment. Damn, she was really rattled. He didn't think he'd ever seen her so—well, livid was probably the right word. The Dragon Lady had never lost her cool like that before.

Derek Simpson had heard stories about her, from her days as an intel analyst at Langley. A lot of people had said she had been tapped to run E&E because of her looks rather than her ability, and there were those who thought the job would be too much for her, too much responsibility.

Maybe they were right.

"And this is what you intend to put in your official report?" she asked angrily.

"Yes, ma'am." He grinned right into her face, watching her as she fought to get herself back under control.

"I'll send a recovery team to your hotel room and get the recordings." She turned away. "For your sake, you better hope they're still there." She headed for the door with the aide hurrying to stay with her.

Derek lay back. *That went exceedingly well*, he thought.

"Contact the retrieval team. I want that hotel room torn apart." He could hear Peterson angrily snapping out orders as she walked away from his room. "And find out the ETA on Noah."

Closing his eyes, Derek started to plan his next moves. He had to make sure he got to talk to Noah before Peterson had a chance to get her claws into him. He needed to make sure that kid had his head on straight before that meeting ever took place.

The door to his room swung open and he looked up, smiling pleasantly at the nurse who had entered to change his dressings. Time to go back to pretending he was a nice guy.

FIVE

They came across an abandoned hunting cabin in a small clearing. The roof had a large, gaping hole in it, all the glass was gone from the windows and the door hung off rusted hinges, but it had four thick stone walls to provide cover and a wooden floor, which meant they could stay off the damp ground. It would do fine as a place to rest up.

While two men stayed back to watch over Noah, the rest of the team had surrounded and then moved in to secure the building. Once they had made sure the place was deserted, the two who had stayed behind carried the wounded assassin inside.

They moved like a well-oiled machine. Each man knew his job and there was no need for Larsen to issue orders. He set a rotation for guard duty and then they settled down quickly to eat, drink and catch up on some much needed rest.

"Hey, Noah, you awake?"

Larsen knelt down next to the injured assassin. Noah had been very quiet ever since their brief conversation earlier. Each time they had stopped, he had watched as Noah had pretended to be asleep while he had replaced the dressing to his head wound and changed the bags of IV fluids and meds.

"Yeah," came the murmured reply.

"Good." He sat down beside him. "So, how are you feeling?"

"I'm fine."

"Yeah, you sound like it," Larsen answered.

Noah swallowed, and for the first time since the morning, made eye contact. "I want to thank you for coming to get me. How did you know where to find me?"

"The men holding you were threatening to parade you on TV for the murder of one of their officials. Your boss lady was raising holy hell about it, so Langley made a point of finding your location." He gave Noah a hint of the trouble waiting for him.

"I didn't—nothing hap..."

Larsen's expression hardened. "You should know something, Noah," he said clearly. "While you were out of it, just after we risked our lives to pull you out of that hole, you talked. You talked a lot."

"I—you—" Noah stuttered as he looked everywhere but at the man facing him.

Larsen gripped the assassin's shoulder, tightening his grip until Noah looked at him. "The death of that man and his family has caused a lot of serious problems back home. You need to pull yourself together. There are a lot of people waiting for answers about what happened in that house." He watched as Noah's face turned to stone. "You need to stop lying to yourself and stop protecting Derek Simpson before he pulls you down with him."

"Derek's alive?" Noah's voice cracked, and he stared at Larsen.

"Last I heard," Larsen answered.

Noah's eyes slid shut. After a moment, Larsen turned away. He couldn't order Noah to speak out against Simpson. He just had to hope he would do the right thing when they got back. Running his fingers through his hair, Larsen rested his back against the wall. Whatever Noah did or didn't do was not his concern. His job was to get the assassin back to base and then his own superiors would decide what to do with him.

NUREMBERG COULD BE A DANGEROUS PLACE, a city dealing with newfound freedoms and the people who try to corrupt them. German police and military patrolled the streets in search of covert Russian agents who were trying to bring back some of the old ways. Many of the shops were shut down. The few that were still open were having a hard time getting merchandise. The only people making money were the black marketeers.

The hotel where they were staying had once been a smart, five star establishment. Now the lack of paying customers had cost them staff and there was no money to keep on top of repairs. The whole place had taken on an air of neglect.

Up on the third floor, Derek was pacing back and forth, his face red with anger.

"He betrayed us," he said. "You heard him, he's planning to sell us out to the Russians. Reitner is a damn traitor. He deserves to die." The knife in his hand suddenly flew through the air, embedding itself in the wooden door.

"So what do we do? Take him out on his way home?" Noah asked from where he sat next to a small writing desk, his hand resting on top of the receiver that had just relayed the bad news. Daniel Reitner was making a deal to turn the two American agents over to the Russians, and for nothing more important than a little extra money.

"No. Go collect the RDX from the safe house." Derek's eyes glinted with malice. "Remember our orders, kid. Nobody is supposed to know we're here. We need to clean this up, and we'll have to collect all the bugs you planted."

"You want to blow the house?" Noah raised an eyebrow. Derek Simpson's reputation indicated a flair for a more personal touch in his operations.

"I want to finish this job and get back to American soil," Derek shot back, his anger still evident. "Never mind that." Derek waved a hand in dismissal. "Just go get the explosives while I sort out the details on how we're gonna clean up this mess."

Noah thought it was at that moment that he knew things were going to get messy, but he had pushed those thoughts away. It was the job. It was what they were paid to do, what they had signed up for.

"Sometimes, it is necessary for one to die to save the lives of many." That was the very reason for the existence of E & E, but people like Simpson preferred to act without such control. Simpson was valuable enough to the CIA that he was allowed to get away with certain things.

Reitner had sealed his fate the second he made a deal to help capture the two American agents. Noah didn't have any problem with killing the man. Reitner had betrayed them, so whatever happened to him was his own fault.

He just hadn't realized how far Derek was going to go. He shouldn't have killed the children, the old folks. They were not any part of the mission, nor of the plot to turn over the Americans to Russia.

No, he wasn't going to think about that. He wasn't there when it happened, he didn't see it. He did nothing.

But now James Larsen was hinting that he might have some idea of the truth.

"You should know, while you were out of it, just after we risked our lives to pull you out of that hole, you talked. You talked a lot."

He remembered Larsen's expression, the look of disappointment and disgust in his eyes. He also remembered the sheer terror on Daniel Reitner's face as Derek's knife plunged into his heart.

Larsen wanted him to report what had happened inside the farmhouse, wanted him to turn on the CIA's number one field operative. The rivalry between E & E and the CIA would turn into an absolute war if he did so.

He felt a tearing sensation and white-hot pain shot through

his scalp. Groaning, Noah opened his eyes while attempting to bat away the fingers probing the sore and inflamed wound.

"Sorry, it's gotta be done," Larsen said as he continued cleaning away the infection that still oozed from the wound. "But we should make it to the extraction point later today and then you're just a chopper ride away from proper medical attention."

"Thank you," Noah said, wincing as a fresh dressing was applied to the back of his head.

"Yeah, well, don't thank me yet. We've got to get through the Russian lines. They're all the way across a ten mile stretch, supposedly on some sort of training exercises." He finished securing the dressing in place and then put everything away. "Think you can manage to eat something?"

"Yeah." At the mention of food, his stomach clenched, as he tried to remember the last time he'd had something to eat. "It's been a while."

Oh, cheer up, kid. I'll buy dinner when we get back to the hotel. Maybe those pretty little waitresses will be on duty in the restaurant, and we can get lucky. Take your mind off of things, right?

"Hey, Noah! Noah, wake up!"

"What?" He looked around, confused by Larsen's concerned expression.

"Keep still."

Noah squinted and tried to look away from the light being shone into his eyes. "What's the matter?"

"You drifted off there for a moment, buddy." Larsen's tone was light, but Noah stared up and caught the worried frown that flickered briefly on the older man's face. "I think we'll pass on giving you something to eat." He looked up through the hole in the roof. "It's nearly daybreak, we'll be moving off soon." He gave Noah a pat on the arm before getting to his feet. "Try to get some rest."

"Larsen?" Noah called out as the older man turned away.

"What?"

"I know you think you know what happened, but it was

necessary. Sometimes there's no other way."Larsen stared down at his feet and then looked the injured spy in the eye. "Is that you talking or Simpson?"

Noah opened his mouth to reply, but then thought better of it. What could he say that would make this right? Larsen would never understand; he worked as part of a team, and while he often had to kill, assassination was not in his job description on a regular basis. There was a structure of command and accountability. He couldn't know what it was like out in the field, where everybody lied, where living or dying was a matter of how quickly you could react, how quickly you could determine who needed to die first.

"I'm tired, I think you're right. I need to rest." Shifting slightly, he closed his eyes. He was already beating himself up about what had happened. He didn't need to hear it from somebody else.

He heard a loud sigh and opened his eyes to find Larsen squatting down at his side. "Noah, I was in Kabul with Derek." He kept his voice low. "I saw how he operates and I know he's pulled some difficult assignments since then, but I can't believe you are going to go along with him when he says that the massacre of a whole family was necessary. You have to say something."

"You weren't there," Noah replied quietly.

"Yeah, well, listening to you rant and rave for six hours made me feel like I was there in that farmhouse with you. Simpson is a lunatic. You won't be held responsible for his actions. Not if you step up."

"Don't worry about it, kid. I've got your back. Anybody says anything, they'll have to deal with me. As far as your boss, I can go right over that bitch Peterson's head. Stick with me and you'll be fine."

Noah closed his eyes and looked away. "I can't. It's like I said before, you wouldn't understand." He lay still, waiting until he heard an annoyed huff and then the creak of rotten floorboards as Larsen moved away. The sounds of the SEAL team getting ready to move out barely registered as Noah worked at pushing the memories of what happened in the farmhouse into the deepest recesses of his mind.

"Ready to go, Noah?"

Noah looked up into the face of one of the SEAL team. He thought the man's name was Barron.

"Yeah." His answer came out as little more than a whisper. He bit down on his lip as he was lifted up and they headed out of the abandoned building and into the thick, early morning mist.

"You sure you're okay, Noah? You look like you're about to pass out."

"I'm fine."

Closing his eyes, Noah willed himself to fall asleep. These men were risking their lives to get him to safety. He wondered if they would be so willing if they knew what he had done. He pushed the thought further away. He had done nothing.

————

NOAH WOKE up to the loud crackle of gunfire, lots of gunfire, some of it coming from close by. While he was still trying to work out what was happening, he suddenly crashed to the ground. Grunting in pain, Noah lay stunned for a moment. The pain radiating from his head wound dimmed his senses, leaving him confused and just briefly filled with fear. He was on a battlefield, wounded and vulnerable.

A bullet hit the ground close to his side, sending up a spray of dirt and grass. It was enough to cause his survival instincts to kick in. Reaching across his body, he pulled out the IV catheter from his arm. He needed to be able to move without dragging tubing and bags of medication around behind him. Then he raised his head just enough to look around.

One of the SEAL team was down, the arm of his fatigues coated in blood. The others were in a semi circle surrounding them, firing into the trees. "Can you move?" Larsen looked back before returning to keeping the hidden enemy back in the trees.

"Yes, sir!" The injured SEAL called back, already raising his rifle one handed to aid his teammates firing on the elusive enemy.

"Noah?" Larsen risked another quick look behind him.

"I think…" Noah attempted to stand, but his legs gave way and the throbbing pain coming from his head wound increased as he tried to move. "No." He hated having to admit it, but now was not the time for lying about his weakness.

"Okay, folks, let's get moving. Barron, help Noah. The LZ is three klicks east and transport is on the way." Noah found himself unceremoniously thrown over Barron's shoulder as the man carried him toward the landing zone. The wounded man kept at their side, holding his rifle awkwardly in one hand, ready to give covering fire if necessary. Behind them, Larsen and the remaining SEALs formed up a rear guard, keeping the advancing men at bay. Looking back, Noah caught sight of a Russian Army uniform. He knew that if they didn't reach the LZ soon, they were going to be in a lot of trouble. The troops would have already called for backup; more soldiers would be flooding the area, and possibly air support too. If the Russians called in their helicopters, the rescue mission would be aborted and they would have to continue to fight their way clear before trying to call for a med evac.

Noah watched as another of Larsen's men took a bullet, his body going limp as he fell back. The remaining SEALs closed ranks around the body. While one man picked up the unconscious man, the others sent several grenades toward their pursuers. Overhead came the welcoming roar of the twin engines of a Blackhawk helicopter, the heavy rotor blades sending up clouds of dust and tearing leaves off the trees. The loud staccato drumbeat of its guns cleared away the Russian troops long enough for it to touch down for the few seconds necessary to allow the SEAL team and Noah to board before rising back to the air and moving away at speed.

As the Blackhawk rose up into the air, Noah was strapped

onto a stretcher. A medic quickly checked his vitals before turning away to help with the two injured SEALs. Left on his own, he stared up at the ceiling, listening to the loud twin engines roar as they gained height, the fast moving blades propelling them out of danger. Pretty soon, he was going to be back on a U.S. airbase and from what Larsen had hinted at, there was going to be a whole lot of people wanting answers from him. Closing his eyes, he realized he was going to have to make a decision on what he was going to say.

SIX

As soon as the Blackhawk touched down at Sigonella, medical teams rushed forward to carry away the wounded. Larsen and the rest of the uninjured SEALs stayed out of the way until their teammates and the spy were safely on their way to the base hospital. Then they slowly made their way toward the armory to get rid of their weapons and on to the barracks for a shower and some well earned sleep.

"Lieutenant Commander Larsen?"

Larsen stopped in his tracks and turned to face a tall, pasty-faced young man dressed in fatigues that looked like they had just come off the shelf and wearing boots with only a thin layer of dust and not a single crease. This was some company office clerk. No, he revised his opinion when he noticed Michael's muscle tone. He was a rookie CIA field agent probably on his first assignment. Which meant he was about to be called into a meeting with whoever had been put in charge of the CIA investigation.

"Whatever it is, it can wait," Larsen growled and began to follow the rest of his men.

"Sir, I've been sent to get you." The young man followed him, jogging to keep up. "I'm E & E Agent Michael Logan. My boss wants to see you now."

"Your boss will have to wait. Tell him I said he needs to remember the chain of command. I report to a whole different..."

"Sir, Director Peterson told me not to take no for an answer." Michael almost ran into Larsen as he came to an abrupt halt.

"Peterson? Allison Peterson?"

"Yes, sir."

Larsen dropped his chin and took a deep breath. "Fine, lead the way." It had been a couple of years since he had last seen Allison Peterson, but he knew damn well that if he ignored the polite request, she would come down to the barracks and drag him back to her office. It was better to give in gracefully.

He walked through the door Logan held open and looked at the woman standing behind her desk.

"Okay, I'm here. What's so damned important you can't wait until..." He halted his words when he saw the look on her face.

Allison stared back at him, her blue blue eyes narrowed in concentration, her mouth set in a thin, tight line. She stared past his shoulder. "You can go, Michael."

She waited for the young agent to close the door to her office. "Sorry, Larsen, but I needed to see you as soon as possible, before the official debriefing."

Dropping his backpack and leaning his rifle against the wall, Larsen slumped down in a chair in front of the desk. "Okay, Allie, what's so important I can't have a shower and a sleep before being dragged in to see you?"

The nickname slipped out naturally. They had known each other for years, from back in Allison's days as a CIA analyst. It was because of that history that he could see the anger and frustration that was bubbling under the cool exterior.

She stepped from behind the desk to stand in front of him. "I need to know if Noah said anything about what happened out there."

No warm greeting, not even a smile of welcome. Things were definitely worse than he had suspected. "He was out of his mind for most of the time. He's got a nasty head injury. In my opinion, he's suffering from some kind of shock, and I—" What else could he say? He had no proof. He just had to hope Noah Wolf had a conscience.

"Shock? What do you mean?"

Larsen shrugged. "Look, Allie, I know who Camelot is. A lot of us in the community know, but the kid I just brought back? There's no way in hell he could be the emotionless, superefficient killer you seem to be so proud of. This boy? His mind is rattled, Allie, and it'll surprise me if he's ever able to go back in the field after this."

She stared at him for several seconds, then let out a sigh. "Larsen, I'm under a lot of pressure to send in my report," she explained. "Questions are being asked at the UN. Russia has accused the U.S. of interfering in another country's politics, while Germany is accusing us of assassinating one of their government officials. Moscow expelled four of our diplomats last night and D.C. is expected to retaliate later today. There could be some serious blowback if this continues to get out of hand. There are even two committees in Congress demanding my organization be shut down immediately."

Allison reached behind her and picked up a thin file. She held it up. "This is Derek Simpson's debrief. He claims that they discovered Reitner was a Russian spy. He expects me to believe he and Noah went out to the Reitner residence to talk. That loose cannon told me that Reitner tried to shoot them and after they had escaped, Reitner blew up his own house, killing himself and his family."

Larsen thought about what he had heard during Noah's delirium-fueled confession. Derek was going to weasel his way out of facing charges for cold-blooded murder. "He went to talk? That doesn't sound like Derek."

Allison paused and looked deeper into Larsen's brown eyes. She knew him very well, well enough to know when he was hiding something. Throwing the file back onto the desk, she began to pace around the office. Simpson was lying to her and now Larsen was hiding something too.

"No, it doesn't, but the CIA loves him and I'm being pressured to accept his report as the official version. He says they left recording equipment at their hotel. I've had it picked up, but it's going to take at least a week to get it verified and by then, if I've signed off on his report and something else comes to light, I'll be the one thrown under the bus." She paused to fix him with a stare, not letting him break eye contact. "If Noah has lost his edge, I could be out on my ass within a month. E & E probably won't survive without me, not for more than a few weeks, anyway. Did he say anything coherent at all?"

"I told you, he was out of his mind most of the time I was with him," Larsen replied, uneasy with the questioning and with the way she was looking at him.

"Look, I know there's more to Simpson's story than he's telling me and whatever it is, I need to know the truth. It's my name that goes on that report and if something comes out later, I'm not letting that son of a bitch ruin my career."

"Have you passed on your concerns?" Larsen hoped to distract her from questioning him further on what Noah had said.

"When he pulled the assignment, I told the President Simpson was the wrong man for it. It was a damn fishing expedition, but there have been questions about Derek's state of mind. The white coats thought a simple recruiting mission might give him a break without taking him out of the field. As much as I hate how the man operates, he usually does get the job done. If this thing does blow up between the Russians and Germany, we're going to need people like those two on the ground."

Larsen looked at Allison and sighed. She deserved to know the truth. "Pour me a shot of the bourbon you've got hidden in that drawer and I'll tell you what I heard."

She eyed him up and down. "I'm not your barmaid now, Lieutenant Commander Larsen."

"You'll always be my barmaid, Allie, and you know it." He managed to pull off a full blown James Larsen charming smile.

She gave him a soft smile in return and went to the drawer he had indicated. James Larsen always seemed to have a knack for knowing where the alcohol was kept. Pouring him a lot more than a shot, she handed him the drink and then turned to perch on the edge of her desk, facing him.

"So what do you know?" she asked, crossing her arms over her chest. She hadn't poured herself a drink. This was business. She took her job very seriously and she wasn't going to let her reputation be ruined because of Derek Simpson.

"It's all hearsay. Noah was out of his mind at the time and I can tell you now, Simpson has gotten deep into his head."

"Spit it out, Larsen," Allison groused. She recognized the signs of Larsen taking on a cause.

"Noah was raving about what sounded like a massacre," he finally spoke. After taking a big gulp of bourbon, he continued. "The way I understood it, Derek sent Noah out of the room and then he killed the whole family. He called Noah back in help him clear up the mess."

Allison paled at the thought. She had suspected for some time that Simpson was heading off the reservation, but she hadn't dreamed that he had gone this far off.

"I'll talk to Noah once the doctors have finished with him and then I'll make a decision on what to do about Derek Simpson."

"There's no proof, Allie. If Noah backs Derek up, what are you going to do?"

"Oh, there'll be something somewhere that I can nail to his hide. Between Derek's last psych report and what just happened, I'll threaten to have him burned. He'll break."

Larsen leaned forward, placing the drink on the table. "Taking it out on Noah is not going to get rid of Derek and you know it. That kid deserves a break. I've worked with Derek, a couple of times. He's a force to be reckoned with. He just steamrollers right over you and he has the backing of the higher ups. How about after you've done your debrief, if he still won't 'fess up, you let me have a go at him."

"You think you can get him to talk?" she asked.

"We have a history. I knew him years ago, worked a couple of jobs with him back when he was a Ranger, then the job in Kabul." He let out a sigh. "Look, even some of his own people have noticed a change in him. At least give him a chance."

Allison looked across the room, lost in her own thoughts. Simpson had been a good agent and his record as a Ranger had been outstanding, but he had changed over the last year. She had read enough of his reports in the past to know the man, and rumors she had been hearing the last year or so were unsettling.

As for Noah, he was the rising star of E & E. It was the name of Camelot the FSB was whispering; the ghost who seemed unstoppable, and managed to do the impossible on almost every mission. If being with Derek got him burned to the point of being out-of-favor, E & E could easily be disbanded, and that wasn't something she could allow to happen. Considering where most of her people had come from, they weren't going to be allowed to walk away into civilian lives. They would end up in a mass grave somewhere, and no one would even know what had happened to them.

"You go get your rest and I'll give you a call after I've spoken to him. It probably won't be until tomorrow. He's in surgery now."

Larsen got to his feet and gently placed his hands on her shoulders. Leaning in, he placed a soft kiss on her forehead. "How about you let me have a shower and get a few hours rest and then I'll come back over and help you run through your debrief." His suggestion was very plain.

She pushed him away, wrinkling her nose. "Make sure you shower at least twice before coming back. You stink."

After Larsen closed the door on his way out, Allison went around the desk and sat down with a sigh. She pulled out Noah

Wolf's file and began to read. She was going to break Simpson and then throw him out on his murderous ass.

———

"CONTACT THE RETRIEVAL TEAM. I want that hotel room torn apart and check the ETA on Noah."

With Peterson gone from his room, Derek lay back in his bed and closed his eyes while he set about analyzing what had just occurred. The Dragon Lady had lost her temper and it had very nearly thrown him. She was angry about Reitner turning out to be a traitor and with them keeping her out of the loop. He suddenly smirked; that had to be it; the little lady didn't like to be made to look foolish. Twice.

Oh, she was definitely going to be pissed at Noah. He needed to make sure he got in to see Noah before Peterson had a chance to get her claws into him. He had been acting a little off ever since he had finished his interrogation of Reitner, so the first item on the agenda was to find out where Noah was being held and find a way in to see him.

He was just trying to work out how he was going to achieve his objectives when the door opened and a young nurse stepped into his room.

"Agent Simpson? Is it alright if I change your dressings?" He had noticed this particular nurse before and had already formed the opinion that she would make an ideal asset. She was young, inexperienced and, by the way she looked at him, had serious daddy issues.

"Well, hey, there, darlin', and how are you today?" He revealed his teeth in a wide, friendly smile.

"I'm fine, Agent Simpson and how about you? Do you need anything?"

"Oh, all I need is for you to call me Derek." He peered at her name tag. "Angie." He noted her eager smile and the faint blush that colored her cheeks. This was going to be so easy. He turned up his smile a notch and watched her blush grow even brighter.

By the time the dressings were changed on his shoulder and hip, she had agreed to let him know when Noah arrived on the base and to keep him informed on his condition. She even agreed to keep it their little secret.

"I can't tell you how much this means to me, Angie." He gently laid his hand on top of hers. "You're an angel." He nearly choked on the words, but they had the desired effect. She left promising to come back as soon as she knew anything.

"Jeez, I just get better with age," he muttered to himself. "Or maybe it's just that the girls get dumber."

With that, he finally let the feeling of exhaustion overtake him and went to sleep. He was confident the little nurse would be back as soon as she had the information he wanted and he was right. By the evening, he knew that Noah had arrived with a SEAL team. He had been taken straight through to surgery with a badly infected head wound and possible blood poisoning. He also had several broken fingers and a couple of cracked ribs.

Digesting the news, Derek came to the conclusion that Peterson would wait until the anesthesia had worn off before attempting to question Noah. He was planning his next move when he felt a soft hand on his wrist. He looked up, just managing to mask his irritation.

"What is it, darlin'?" Why was she hanging around?

"I'll see you later—Derek." She spoke in a breathy little voice that set his teeth on edge.

"Remember, you promised to get me in to see Noah as soon as he's out of surgery. It's really important to me."

"B-but my shift." Her words dried up as he stared at her; all this sweet talk was grating on his nerves. Behind his smile and hopeful expression, Derek was thinking that he could easily snap her neck with his one good hand. He flexed his fingers as his eyes dropped to her throat. She was a skinny thing; yes, he could definitely kill her with one hand.

"Derek, are you listening to me?"

He realized he was daydreaming. "Sorry." He gasped, shifting as if in pain. "My leg. What is it, honey?"

"I said I'll call back in a couple of hours when it's a bit quieter. I should be able to sneak you in to see him then." She paused at the door. "I won't get into trouble for this, will I?"

"No, it will be fine," he said, smiling for her again. "I promise."

As the door swung shut, the charming smile fell from Derek's face, replaced by a scowl. God, lonely women were so damn easy. Show them a bit of attention and they were all over you. It was boring.

SEVEN

NOAH FELT THE JOLT AS THE HELICOPTER LANDED, AND then the sensation of being transported rapidly out into the open and into a cool, well lit building. He was aware of all the hustle around him, the multitude of voices all becoming one confusing, disorienting noise. He struggled briefly against the hands removing his clothing and pulling him about, but then he felt himself begin to slip away.

Then came the rancid scent of death and faintly, James Larsen's voice whispering in his ear.

"Simpson is a lunatic," he was saying. "give him up, Noah, you won't be held responsible for his actions. Not if you step up."

Held responsible? "I didn't do anything wrong."

The smell of death and dying was getting stronger. He could hear pitifully whimpering voices and the soft noise of a silenced weapon being fired into flesh. One, two, three. He stopped counting.

"You tell him, kid. What we do saves lives. All Langley cares about is the end result. They don't want to know all the dirty little details." Derek looked down at his blood soaked shirt. "When we get back to civilization, we're going to need to take a trip to the tailors. This was my last decent shirt."

Bodies were piling up before his eyes, some had had it coming, some were a case of being in the wrong place, mixing with the wrong people, and some didn't deserve it at all.

A teddy bear lay on the kitchen floor.

"I can't believe it was necessary to massacre that whole family, Noah. You have to say something." There was Larsen again, the voice of reason.

"Reason? Don't tell me you're listening to Larsen. Remember Kabul, kid. He's not like us. He'd never cut it in our world."

"You weren't there and you wouldn't understand. You work under different rules of engagement. What we do, me and Derek, is not the same as working in the teams."

Reitner was a traitor, both to America and to his own people. He had betrayed them. He was about to sell them both out to the FSB for money. He deserved what he got.

The children, he could hear them, see them, laughing, playing outside, chasing the chickens that ran loose in front of the house. The old woman sat on a chair shelling peas, her cackling laugh drawing his attention on the day they first visited the Reitner home.

"You shouldn't have killed the children, Derek."

"Maybe you're just not cut out for this. Maybe the Dragon Lady got it wrong and you really don't belong in this job." Derek raised an eyebrow as he casually buried the hilt of his knife into Daniel Reitner's chest.

"Noah? Noah? Can you hear me? You're out of surgery. Everything went well and you are going to be fine."

A comforting hand was resting on his shoulder. "Lay still and just press this if you need assistance." His hand was wrapped around a device, his thumb placed over the top. "We'll take you to your room in a little while."

He blinked and tried to talk, but instead of words, he coughed and groaned. Surgery. He was back.

The death of that man and his family has caused a lot of heat back home. You need to pull yourself together. There are a lot of people wanting answers about what happened in that house. You need to stop lying to yourself and stop protecting Derek Simpson before he pulls you down with him."

"It's called wet work for a reason, kid. Maybe you should just call the Dragon Lady and tell her you wanna go home to Mommy."

Pain, searing pain, shot through his head and his eyes flew open.

"Hey, kid." He heard the words as if they were coming from a long way off.

More pain and the voice was louder, angrier. He could just make out a large shape looming over him.

"Dad?"

"No, kid. C'mon, this is important."

"Derek?" Finally he could identify the face of his nightmare beaming down at him.

"Nice of you to join me, kid."

"D-Derek?" Noah groaned. He looked around in confusion. He was out of the post op ward and in what appeared to be a small side room.

"Yeah, kid. Now, we only have a short time. You're in big trouble."

"I'm what?" Noah was still trying to make sense of what had happened. How could he be in trouble?

Derek was shaking his head, pretending sympathy. "That bitch Peterson is heading the investigation into the mission and man, is she pissed off at you."

"At me? Why?" Noah's eyes went in and out of focus. "Allison?" Why would Allison be angry at him?

"Jeez, kid, pull yourself together. She tried to get rid of you after your Andropov operation, don't you remember?"

Andropov, he remembered Andropov. That was the night he almost died. He had gone up against the most deadly killer in the world and beaten him, taking back what the son of a bitch had taken from him. Sarah, he had taken Sarah...

The rush of pride fell away as he was suddenly assailed with images of the farmhouse.

"She—" She had slapped him down after Andropov; he vaguely remembered wondering briefly if she was going to take him away from his team, but she hadn't.

"Damn it, concentrate!" Derek slapped his hands down on the railing around the bed. He was losing his patience. "She's already taken my preliminary report, you've just got to remember things the same way I did."

"Derek, you—we killed..." The image of the bodies piled up on the floor came back to him. It could have been a scene from Bosnia, or Kabul, but it wasn't.

"Do you really think anybody is interested in knowing how we got the job done?" Derek hissed angrily. "All that matters is that we did!"

"No." He didn't have to think about the answer. Even after all the things he had done, or had seen done, not once had he been asked to tell everything that happened. Except by Allison Peterson.

"That's right, kid. They don't care about the details, only the results, but you fouled up big time. You got caught, but we can work this out, put the blame where it really belongs."

Noah wearily wiped a hand over his eyes; he was having trouble staying awake. The images in his mind were mingling with reality. The first time he saw a mass grave was in Afghanistan, a whole community wiped out, except for a small group of women who spent what remained of their days wishing they were with the rest of their families. It took months to finally hunt down their target, and after a week, he had seen so many horrors that he was glad he wasn't able to be shocked.

"Noah, are you listening to me? You say the wrong thing and you'll be out. I won't be able to save your butt if you don't stick with me. That whiny little traitor tried to get the drop on us, we fought our way out and then his house blew. Got it?"

"I didn't do anything." He was coming around more now. Derek's urgent tone was forcing him to concentrate.

"That's right, you didn't do anything. It was Reitner. He got the drop on us and after we escaped, he blew up his own house." Derek repeated his version of events again.

"But..."

"Don't you get it? It was the CIA's asset who was the traitor; it was the CIA's asset who blew the house. Neither of us did anything wrong. We were lucky to get out in one piece and get back to pass on the intel."

"Derek, civilians died. You, you killed... "

Derek gave an impatient sigh. "What was the mission brief?" Noah grimaced as the pain in his head worsened. "To find out which leaders in the German government would be most open to revealing discussions between Germany and Russia."

Noah nodded groggily. "Yeah..."

"And what were the orders regarding our presence?"

Noah licked his lips. "Nobody was to know of our presence."

"So we did what we had to."

"They were children," Noah answered softly.

"Children who would have told the German authorities that we spoke to their father, that we killed their father. You do understand that Reitner had to die? He was a traitor; he was going to get us killed. How many lives did we save by stopping him from betraying his own people?"

Noah was tired, still under the effects of the anesthesia and his head was hurting worse than before. He knew Derek wasn't going to drop it until he agreed. A little part of him even thought Derek had a point.

"Peterson wants us both to go down, you know that. She can't handle all the responsibility and she's trying to put the blame on us when she gets caught up in something that can ruin things for her."

Noah didn't try to argue the point; instead he gave a slight nod, wincing at the pain the movement caused.

"It was their asset. The CIA told us to use Reitner."

"You said Reitner was your asset."

"Only because they gave him to me. If you look at it the right way, you'll see it's all their fault." He grinned now, a fatherly smile of encouragement. "I know you did the best you could, kid. You didn't set out to get captured, but Peterson—I don't think she sees it that way. You don't need to distract from the job we did by going into details. Reitner got what he deserved and he might as well have blown his own house up." He waited to see what effect his words would have.

"Okay," he whispered.

"I knew you would come around." Derek beamed. He looked up at the clock on the wall. "Now, my ride will be back in a few minutes. Let's go through what you're going to say to the Dragon Lady while we wait."

———

LEAVING ALLISON'S OFFICE, Larsen had made his way across the compound. Glancing over at the hospital, he wondered if there was any news about his men. Garvey's wound hadn't looked too serious, just a very bloody and messy flesh wound, but Alonzo, well, he had been hit hard. A bullet hit him just below the hem of his bulletproof vest, a nasty gut wound. The kid had been lucky that it happened only minutes before the chopper had arrived with a trained medical crew.

Larsen paused as if he was going to turn and go to the hospital, but then changed his mind. It was only an hour since they had reached the base. He doubted there would be any news yet.

Reaching the barracks, it took him only a few minutes to find his team's sleeping quarters. He wasn't surprised to find that the remaining members were sitting up, waiting for his return.

"Noah's boss wanted to know how her boy was doing," he told them. "You all should get some shut eye. I'm gonna get a shower and then head over to the hospital."

As he was gathering up his shower bag and a clean set of fatigues, he heard a snigger and then Lonnie Gordon, whom he had known since SEAL training, asked a question. "The spook's commander wouldn't happen to be a dirty blonde ex-CIA analyst?"

Larsen stopped for a moment before turning back to his men. "That's classified information, Lonnie." Walking away, he could hear the other men asking Gordon about a certain ex-CIA analyst who had graduated to running her own organization.

A few minutes later, he was under a hot shower, washing away all the sweat and grime from three long days in the wilderness. He really didn't envy Allison the job of trying to burn Derek Simpson. He wondered briefly if it might have been better for all concerned if he had just kept his mouth shut. He had gotten a strong impression that Noah Wolf wasn't going to give up his mission partner that easily. Drying himself off, he got dressed in the freshly laundered fatigues and searched through his wash kit for his razor.

Maybe this was what Noah needed, somebody like a pissed off Allison Peterson on his ass. He had seen her in action several times in the past. Camelot wasn't going to stand up to her, Larsen was sure of that.

He checked himself out in the mirror. Maybe he would find the time for a little debriefing session after visiting the hospital. He had told her he would call back later.

Feeling a bit more human after a shower and shave, Larsen found a table and chair and wrote out his report, trying to remember all the details of the extraction and the shooting of his teammates. By the end of it all, he was rubbing at his tired, bloodshot eyes. It was the part of the job he hated, all the reports at the end of any mission. A glance at his watch told him that enough time had passed that if all had gone well, both men should be out of surgery.

The hospital was quiet, the corridors empty. The only sign of life was around the nurses' station. He stopped at the surgery ward, inquiring after his men. As he stood chatting, he happened to glance along one of the corridors. His eyes narrowed as he watched a familiar shape in a wheelchair leaving a side room.

"Who's in the third room along on the right?" he asked, pointing along the corridor.

The nurse glanced at the chart she was holding, showing the patients on her ward. "Wolf, Noah—oh, he came in with you, didn't he?"

She was left talking to his back as Larsen strode down the corridor and entered the room just vacated by Derek Simpson.

Noah was laying on his side, his head covered by a thick dressing. He looked up at his latest visitor through tired eyes.

"Hey, Noah," Larsen said as he entered the room. "How are you doing?"

"I'm tired," he answered flatly.

"I'll bet. Was that Derek I just saw being wheeled away?" He pulled a chair from the corner of the room, sitting down beside Noah's bed.

"Yeah. Look, Larsen, I'm really tired and..." He let the sentence fade away, hoping Larsen would take the hint.

"That's okay, buddy. I was calling in to check on my two men who were shot getting you back here. One of them is gonna be fine, by the way. The other, well, I'm not so sure about the other one. Thank you for asking."

Noah blinked. "I meant to ask, but..."

"But you're too busy learning the lines Derek just fed you. Am I right?"

Noah looked as guilty as hell. "He just came to see me, that's all."

Larsen sighed. What he wanted to do was shake the younger man until he understood he was following the lead of a psychopath, but he also knew shouting at Noah would get him nowhere. So instead he settled for a bit of sarcasm. "Yeah, that's Derek, always looking out for everybody."

Noah closed his eyes. "I'm sorry about your men."

"But not about the murder of women and children?"

"That's unfair," Noah said, "and it's also something you

know nothing about." He took a shaky, deep breath. "I need to get some sleep, Larsen. Can we continue this tomorrow?"

"Yeah, sure." Larsen got to his feet, placing the chair back where it came from. "Noah, I know you're only listening to one person at the moment, but can you just think about this? If Derek gets away with what he's done this time, what's he going to ask you to cover up next?"

EIGHT

E & E Director Allison Peterson was still sitting at her desk when she got word that Noah was out of surgery and expected to make a full recovery. She looked at her wristwatch; it was after ten p.m. She had been staring at the mission file for three hours and was no further along. There was one thought that kept playing in the back of her mind. Noah Wolf had been her very best.

She had given the young assassin a number of seemingly impossible missions since she had recruited him. He was undoubtedly the superstar of her organization, the man who always got things done and always came back. He was smart, worked well under pressure, had a knack for becoming whoever he needed to be for a mission and, when he wanted to, he had an easy charm that made people open up to him.

But that had been before she had been forced to send him off with Derek Simpson. It was before their mission blew up into something that could cause enough international incidents to be a forerunner of World War III.

Pushing the file across the desk, she leaned back in her chair. Screwing up her eyes, she pinched the bridge of her nose. Just the possibility of losing Noah was enough to make her feel ill. It also focused her misgivings about the two men lying injured in the base hospital.

But if what Larsen had told her was true, this time it was a lot worse. If Noah's delusional ramblings were to be believed, then Simpson had executed a whole household, men, women and children. Every one of them had been a civilian, and it looked like Noah had helped him destroy the evidence.

She sat forward again. There was no way she was going to sign off on that mission until she had the truth. It was a damned CIA mission to begin with, and she had resisted when they asked for Noah to go out with Simpson on it, but Alex Walker, the CIA Director, had gone to the president. She had been ordered to send Noah along, and there was nothing she could do about it.

But now that it had gone sour, Walker was trying to dump all of the blame on Noah. If Simpson managed to keep Noah on his side, it was going to blow up in her face, but she wasn't about to let that happen.

Simpson wasn't getting away with it. She would keep him away from Noah, isolating them until she found out what Noah actually knew.

"Michael!" She went to the door and smiled at the man still at his desk. "Put a call through to the hospital. When Noah is ready to leave post op, have him put in a single room as far away from Simpson as possible, and then arrange for a guard to be put on both of their rooms."

As she finished speaking, she noticed James Larsen standing in the doorway to the outer office.

"Larsen." She smiled over at him, noticing he had followed her advice and was clean, groomed and dressed in fresh clothes. "Come on in." She beckoned him into her office.

Once inside, she closed the door and turned to face him. Staring at her with solemn eyes, he gently cupped her shoulders.

"I heard what you said out there, but you're too late, Allie. I went past Noah's room and saw Derek being wheeled away down the corridor."

LARSEN LEFT Noah's room and headed straight for Allison's office. He was going to have to find a way of suggesting that if she wanted to get Noah Wolf to 'fess up to what had happened in that German farmhouse, she needed to tighten up her security measures.

He reached her outer office, his fingers closing around the handle when he heard her voice coming from inside.

"Michael! Put a call through to the hospital. When Noah is ready to leave post op, have him put in a single room as far away from Simpson as possible and then arrange for a guard to be posted on their rooms."

Taking a deep breath, he opened the door, stopping just inside the room. She looked across at him, her eyes flickering over his clean shaven features and freshly laundered fatigues.

With a welcoming smile on her lips, she beckoned him to follow her. "Larsen. Come on in." He watched her carefully as she stiffened before shrugging his hands off her shoulders and turning her back on him. "This is exactly what I said would happen. If you're right about what happened at Reitner's, then Simpson has gone rogue, and he may have dragged Noah down with him. I'm going to have to shut him down before he ends up killing more civilians and bringing my own agency down in the process." She began to pace around the room, her eyes narrowed as she tried to think her way through the fiasco before her.

Larsen watched as Allison completed a circuit of her office. He knew that if he let her, she would keep going until she either came up with an answer or dropped from exhaustion. Taking the matter into his own hands, he caught hold of her around the waist and guided her to a chair.

"Larsen, do I have to..." Anger flared in her eyes at his presumption.

He held up a hand to stop the words about to come from her mouth while he pulled up another chair and sat down facing her.

"I know you're frustrated, but wearing a hole in the floor isn't going to fix the problem, Allie. You know if you're going to break Derek's hold over Noah, you can't go in angry. Derek's got his tendrils wrapped tight around Noah, he's in his head. I could tell that by the way the kid got so defensive whenever I asked what happened."

"This mission was important. If the Russians get a foothold inside the German government, the entire European Union could be in danger. Instead of doing what they were supposed to do, they traveled into areas they had no business entering, failed to keep their contacts informed of their whereabouts and, if the stories I'm hearing are true, they have both committed unsanctioned eliminations. My detractors will use this information to claim that they are completely out of control, and that Noah is just as bad as Simpson."

Larsen stared at her. He had heard all the rumors circulating; spies really were a bunch of bitchy little girls talking about each other behind each others' backs.

"Everyone knows that Camelot is a code name for a special E & E team that gets the dirtiest missions. Is that why you sent him with Simpson? I heard about him at Langley, after what happened with Nicolaitch Andropov."

She raised an eyebrow, not terribly surprised about how far the story had spread.

"Noah went in to get one of his team, take her back from Andropov." She smiled at the only bright spot of that mission. "In the course of it, he damn near got himself killed."

Larsen just looked at her. "How?"

"Andropov had taken her prisoner. He used her as bait to lure Noah into a trap, but Noah turned the trap around on him. In the course of escaping, Noah was shot several times and ended up with a knife through his hand. He still came back with the girl."

"Oh, man, what I'd'a given to see that." Larsen chuckled. "I don't suppose you've still got the mission photographs handy?"

"Those pics are classified, Larsen."

"Yeah, but they're in his file, right? I promise not to tell—just a peek." He leaned back in his chair and winked.

"Larsen, you're not helping me here." She smiled back at him though, grateful for the break in the tension.

"Oh, come on, please? I could always brag I saw the famous Camelot at his worst."

"Sounds to me," she said, "like you can say that now. My big problem is Derek Simpson. The only way I can get rid of that problem is if Noah decides to come clean on what happened in Germany, and from you've just told me, that's not going to happen." She was back on her feet again. "I've got to find some way to make sure Derek doesn't get the chance to pull the strings this time."

"Hey, easy, Allie," Larsen said. "Noah's just a kid and Derek's got him all messed up. You didn't see him out there. Some of what he went through out there might have caused some brain damage, and that might be why he was yelling his head off about what went on in that farmhouse. I'm telling you, whatever Derek did out there made Noah absolutely sick."

Allison shook her head. "You don't know Noah, James," she said. "That isn't possible. Noah Wolf is incapable of being made sick by anything he might see. He suffers from a disorder that leaves him without emotions. He has no conscience, no fear and absolutely no revulsion reflex."

LARSEN'S EYEBROWS WENT UP. "Are you serious? Allie, I watched him crying like a baby, the whole time mumbling about how the children shouldn't have died. Every time I looked at his face, there was nothing but grief on it. This guy is about as emotionless as a Hallmark card."It was Allison's turned to stare. "James," she said, "you have to be mistaken. There's no way Noah Wolf is going to cry, let alone display any emotion."

"Then something happened to your guy," Larsen said. "I'm telling you, he acted like he was having some kind of nervous breakdown. Crying, mumbling to himself, and anytime I tried to talk to him about it, he either got angry or just started sulking."

Allison shook her head. "Oh, dear God," she mumbled. "If you're telling me the truth, Noah may be ruined forever. He was my superstar, Larsen. He was the best we ever had, which is why he only got the worst missions, of course." She shook her head again. "I should've told Walker to go to hell when he asked for Noah to go with Simpson on this mission. I knew something was off, I just couldn't imagine it would go this bad."

Larsen rolled his eyes. "Allie, you're talking about Derek Simpson. If you look in the dictionary for the definition of disaster, it'll be his picture that you find. I would never work with Simpson again if I had any choice in the matter. Nothing short of a direct order can get me to so much as have lunch with that bastard."

"Walker swears by him," Allison said. "Apparently, they think he's the best CIA has."

Larsen snorted. "If you ask me, you should seriously consider ordering a sanction on Derek Simpson. He's bad, Allie."

"You think I don't know that?" she snapped. "You're not talking to an amateur, here, Larsen." She'd had enough of that sort of patronizing talk from Derek Simpson. She didn't like excess familiarity, not even from somebody as close to her as Larsen had once been, but what he had said had taken away almost her last tiny bit of hope for the young assassin. If he had truly been sickened by what Derek had done, however, then his usefulness might be at an end as far as E & E was concerned.

"You know, Noah has been the bright spot in my whole organization, ever since I first recruited him. Without him, we can't be nearly as effective. The trouble is that it was his lack of emotion that made him the best, so if he's truly giving in to an emotional response, he may be done."

She suddenly paled as another thought struck her. Despite all of this, she was going to have to take the time to call home to

Neverland and update Sarah and the others. She owed them that much, at least.

She sat down heavily again, staring up at Larsen with a determined expression. "You served with Derek. Tell me about Kabul; not the official report, but what actually happened there."

Larsen took a deep breath and sat down facing her. "You read the reports?" he asked.

She stared back at him. "Of course," she said. "I've read everything I could find on this son of a bitch, ever since I found out how bad things had gotten out there."

"Okay, jeez," Larsen said. He felt a bit like a school boy telling tales.

He thought about how much he should tell her. She wasn't going to want to know about how he made contact with the two spies, though that first meeting certainly showed him how much Derek had changed since the last time he had seen him.

He had found Simpson and his partner waiting for him inside an abandoned cottage, Derek's eyes glaring at him through the darkness. Another hunched figure crouched by the empty fireplace, looking like he was ready to pounce. It had only been when Derek had turned up the wick on an old oil lamp that he had noticed the blood and dirt staining the clothes of two men; no, not just their clothes, but their skin and hair, as well. There had been an air about both of them of barely contained violence.

Derek had insisted that they wait until the moon had risen high in the sky and all traces of daylight had vanished before leading the way toward General Fassad's camp. Larsen remembered how shocked he had been when they climbed over the crest of a hill and he got his first look at what the other two men had been dealing with for the last few months.

His senses had reeled at the stench coming from a pile of dead bodies near the entrance to the camp, apparently just left there to rot. Further in, they had passed by a drunken crowd cheering and jeering as the body of a man, hopefully dead, was dragged behind a motorcycle, and then there were the sobs and cries of the women. Larsen closed his eyes, not wanting to allow those memories back to the surface. He had been there for less than twenty-four hours; Derek and his trainee, Gary Phillips, had lived in that camp for months before his arrival.

He remembered the terrified scream of a woman that had sent his hand straying to his weapon. Gary had leaned in close to him, stopping him from drawing the handgun.

"Don't react, you can't help them. Not without blowing our cover." Gary had hissed out the warning, then let go of his arm and moved ahead to keep pace with Simpson. Larsen had walked behind them, wondering how the two men had managed to cope with what they were seeing every day and not go insane.

"Larsen?"

Allison snapped him back to the present and he looked up at her again. "Yeah—sorry. You know what went on there, so, you must have some idea of the things Derek had to have done. He was there for how long? Six months, I think that was right."

She nodded. "Yes, that was during my tenure as an analyst. I have a good idea of what happened, and I saw personally how it affected Phillips. I tried to get him to accept a transfer to analysis or, if he wanted to stay in the field, to find him another agent to work with, but he refused to consider either offer."

She paused, remembering something that had concerned her at the time, something that hadn't rung true during their mission debriefing. At the time, her concerns had been swept under the rug by her section chief. Simpson was an experienced agent and the two men were a successful team. "Stop looking for trouble" had been the final stark warning.

"Do you know what happened to Anton Rosenka?" She stared as Larsen paled. Seeing his face, she knew that it was another case of Simpson going against orders. "Larsen, what happened? Their orders had been to locate him and bring him in for questioning, but they said he died during the extraction of General Fassad."

"Oh yeah, he died alright," Larsen snorted.

"What's that supposed to mean?"

Pausing in the shadows, Derek pointed to a large tent. "Inside is the man we think is Fassad. You ID him and then stay out of the way while me and Gary handle it."

"How are you going to do that?" *he hissed. There had to be close to five hundred heavily armed men in the camp.*

"Leave it to us," *Gary replied a little too eagerly for his liking.*

"C'mon." *Derek urged him to move, leaving Phillips behind. "In ten minutes, Gary is going to set off a diversion and we're going to leave with the general."*

"What about your mission? I thought you weren't to do anything."

Derek laughed. "Two birds with one stone, that's all. Our little arms dealer is going to help us out with our extraction of Fassad."

Ten minutes later, there was a scream and a man came running seemingly out of nowhere with explosives strapped to his chest. Before anybody could help him, he disappeared in a massive fireball.

While the militia still was reeling from the surprise attack, more explosions went off, adding to the chaos and confusion that was spreading rapidly throughout the camp.

"See?" *Derek slapped him on the back as he led the way inside the tent.*

NINE

"LARSEN, ANSWER THE DAMN QUESTION!" ALLISON'S voice brought him back again.

"Sorry." Larsen wiped a hand over his eyes. "I believe they used Rosenka as a decoy to get Fassad out of the camp."

Allison dropped her head down. It was what she had expected to hear.

"The job I put Gary in for after Kabul, I was hoping that getting him away from Derek and talking about what happened on his own would turn him away from the kind of mistakes they'd made, but I guess it was too late." She shook her head, but Larsen wasn't sure whether it was in disgust or defeat. "You know, he spent the next four months acting like a spoiled brat and then, just when I thought Gary was coming around, I find out Simpson had managed to organize regular radio communications between them." She sighed. "Gary Phillips was called on the carpet about it. He was supposed to report to his Station Chief the following morning, but they found him hanging in one of the buildings near where he was staying. Everything indicated suicide, but I always wondered."

Larsen rubbed his eyes, a sudden feeling of tiredness coming over him. "Look, it's pretty obvious whatever is going on with

Noah isn't going to go away while he's under Derek's thumb. Talk to him in the morning; hell, threaten him if you think that will help, but if he still won't give up Derek, before you throw him out into the cold, let me take a run at him. Maybe I can get him to see sense."

She studied Larsen's worn out expression, the depressed look in his eyes.

"C'mon." Thinking about Derek Simpson and how he might have ruined Noah Wolf had given her the beginning of a massive migraine. She got to her feet and offered him her hand to help him up. "You're right. We're just going 'round in circles here. Noah can wait till morning."

She eyed him up and down, noticing the way he was standing, holding more of his weight on his right leg. "Your knee is acting up again." It wasn't a question.

"Coupla aspirin'll take care of the swelling," Larsen answered.

"A massage will take care of the 'swelling' quicker." She smiled.

"A massage, huh? Hm, you sure want to make the swelling go away, Allie? I mean—"

"Shut up, Larsen." She looked at him for a moment, then picked up her cell phone. "Wait outside for a minute. I have a call I have to make."

Larsen stared at her for a second, then shrugged and stepped out of the office. Allison dialed a number from memory and closed her eyes as she put the phone to her ear.

The seven hour time difference meant that it was only five a.m. back at Neverland, but Sarah answered the phone on the first ring.

"Allison? Is he..."

"He's alive, Sarah," Allison said. "He's in bad shape and just came out of surgery, but he's alive." She licked her lips, stalling a moment before she went any further. "The problem—the problem, Sarah, is that he seems to be suffering some sort of emotional breakdown. I'm afraid it's possible that whatever happened to him has broken through the trauma that left him the way we knew him. If that's true…"

She heard the sob through the phone, and knew that Sarah had come to the same conclusion. If Noah had lost his emotionless nature, his usefulness to the organization could be at an end. Unfortunately, there was no provision for anything like a medical discharge from E & E. Those who failed training or became useless for whatever reason had a tendency to disappear. It was an unfortunate necessity of the organization, to protect the secret of its existence.

If Noah were to be incapable of continuing as an assassin, Allison might have no choice but to order his own termination.

———

NOAH WOKE up when an orderly drew the curtains back from over the small window in his room. As he lay there, he noticed one of the little touches that showed Director Peterson had taken charge. Standing in the corner of his room, dressed in guard military BDU's, was a younger man he didn't recognize.

"Hey, I hope I haven't kept you up all night." Noah smiled at the man.

He waited, but got no response to his greeting; definitely a guard. Derek was right. The director was definitely unhappy. He bit his lip. A guard in his room meant she must have found out about Derek's late night visit, but how?

A sudden sinking feeling settled in his gut. James Larsen; the old SEAL was interfering again.

Noah closed his eyes. Every time the SEAL and Derek came together in his thoughts, it left him with a raging headache.

He needed a distraction. The two men weren't even in the room and yet somehow they were battling away inside his head. Shutting off the part of his brain Derek and Larsen were using as their personal combat zone, Noah turned his attention to the only distraction in the room.

"Do you get paid by the hour?" He threw out the comment just to see if he could get any sort of rise out of the man. Nothing. The guard remained motionless.

"Just remember what I told you. Stick with me, kid, and I guarantee we'll get a commendation for neutralizing Reitner."

It was all very well and good for Derek to make these promises, but it wasn't him that Allison Peterson was about to rake over the coals. Allowing his eyes to close, Noah did his best to convince the guard that he was unconcerned by his presence.

By mid-day, and still with no sign of Peterson, Noah concluded that she was deliberately keeping him waiting, trying to wear him down. Well, he'd learned a long time ago that it was a waste of time to worry about the inevitable. To be precise, it had been the day his dad killed his mother, and then turned the gun on himself.

When the door finally swung open and E & E Director Allison Peterson stepped inside, he was surprised to feel a small wave of relief wash over him; at least the waiting was finally over. Now he'd find out what all this was going to mean for the future.

He watched warily as she walked toward him, her back ramrod straight, her hair pulled back tightly. He guessed if she turned around, he would see a thick strand of dirty blonde hair lying between her shoulder blades. She stared down at him, standing with her arms crossed over her chest, her blue eyes cool and flat.

Behind her, her aide stood holding a clipboard; the kid's eyes were firmly fixed on the paperwork in his hands.

"Noah," she said. "I understand you've already had one visitor since surgery." She spoke in a clipped tone. "So I'm not going to bother to ask you about what happened in Daniel Reitner's home. Instead, I want you to explain to me why you fled in the face of the enemy, leaving a wounded colleague behind."

"What?" Noah tried to sit up, but the pain lancing through his head made him fall back gasping. He hadn't expected this.

"Did you or did you not leave Agent Simpson after he was shot?" Allison asked coldly.

"It wasn't..." He wanted to tell her that stopping hadn't been an option, but she was pressing on with her questions.

"I don't want excuses. Answer the question."

He looked at her for a brief second, and then nodded once. "Yes, I did."

She returned the nod.

"You acknowledge leaving Agent Simpson to fend for himself after witnessing him take fire?"

"I was going to come back for him. I was unarmed and severely outnumbered. I..." He closed his eyes as the pain in his head intensified.

"You lost your weapon, abandoned your partner and then managed to get yourself captured. Have I missed anything so far?"

"I..." he began, but she wasn't listening, wasn't interested in hearing his explanation.

"This is not looking good for you, Noah. Perhaps we need to start with a full review of all your recent failures and deficiencies."

You have to kill the Dragon Lady with kindness, kid. Once you lose your temper, she's won. You do not want to get your ass handed to you by some overachieving bitch, do ya?

Noah took a couple of deep breaths, trying to collect his thoughts, but the pain was making it hard to concentrate.

He watched as she picked up a chair from the corner of the room and sat down, crossing one leg over the other as she took the clipboard from her aide.

"Michael, you can leave us now."

Noah lifted his gaze to watch her aide leave the room and noticed for the first time that the guard had also gone.

Now that they were alone, Allison turned over the first page of the stack of paper attached to the clipboard.

"Let's talk about what really happened in Germany. I want to hear your version of events from when you arrived at the home of Daniel Reitner."

She stared at his pale, drawn features. She could see that she had rattled him, but as soon as he opened his mouth, she knew she had lost.

"When we entered the farmhouse, Reitner and his men took us by surprise..."

She held up a hand, stopping his well rehearsed speech. "Three civilians were beyond your skills, Noah? Do you honestly expect me to believe that?"

He stopped and looked at her, but didn't open his mouth. There was something wrong with this situation, but he couldn't quite put his finger on it, and he was reluctant to speak until he figured out what it was.

She smiled graciously, noticing his discomfort, but she was far from done with Camelot. "Please, continue."

Noah's hand strayed to his head, gently probing the thick pad covering the wound to the back of his skull. He knew what he had to do. He was an experienced operative. His cover was being questioned. An inexperienced agent would fold in the face of Director Peterson's hard-eyed gaze, but not him; he was no rookie hotshot fresh off the farm. He knew that when your cover was about to be blown, you played your role even harder.

He straightened his shoulders and forced his thoughts into order before fixing his boss with a steady gaze. The story he'd committed to memory began to flow out again.

"They caught us by surprise. We didn't want to start a blood-bath, so we waited for an opportunity to escape. When we got away, Reitner must have realized that he was going to be outed as a Russian spy."

The soft sound of a silenced handgun being fired on the other side of a thick wooden door, the smell of death, and the image of bodies piled high in the corner of a rustic kitchen.

"So, he rounded up his family and staff and then he blew up his own home, using a high explosive?" She raised an eyebrow at the improbability of her statement.

"He must have thought he had no choice," Noah said. "I mean, the Germans would have killed him if they had found out."

"Yes, it's always amazed me what some people will do when they think they have no choice." She slipped her pen into the holder attached to the clipboard. "The civilian casualty rate just keeps going up when Derek is around, doesn't it?"

"Ma'am?"

"Just an observation, Noah." She got to her feet. "Now, I am going back to my office to go over my notes before writing up my final report. I suggest you think things over very carefully before the official debrief."

"I don't have to think about it," he responded without hesitation.

She regarded him with a cold, hard stare. "As soon as the medical team here gives you the all clear, we're going back to Neverland. Noah, I intend to call for a full performance review and psych evaluation. This time, Agent Simpson will not be present to hold your hand."

"I haven't done anything..." His composure almost seemed to take a small crack.

Don't worry about it. The Dragon Lady is playing you. Stick with me, kid. I can keep you safe. I tell ya, we'll walk away with commendations at the very least.

"That will be for the review board to decide."

She walked out the door, leaving without another word.

Noah stared up at the ceiling, watching the lazy turn of the ceiling fan over his head. A sudden feeling of bile rising in his throat had him reaching for a bowl beside his bed.

"If Derek gets away with what he's done this time, what's he going to ask you to cover up next?" James Larsen's warning rang clearly in his head, but Noah pushed it away.

Sinking back on his bed, he closed his eyes. "I didn't do anything, wasn't even there." He repeated the mantra as he fell into an exhausted sleep. "I didn't do anything, wasn't even there. I didn't do anything, wasn't even there. I didn't do anything."

TEN

Outside Noah's room, Allison spoke to the guard she had placed on the door. "Nobody goes in that room except medical personnel, and when they go in, you go in too, regardless of what they say."

She didn't have any idea who might be helping Simpson, but when she found that person, she was going to make sure he or she was on the next plane Stateside. Maybe she couldn't bring charges, but there were other ways to deal with traitors and spies.

Walking away with the clipboard clasped tightly in her hand and a stony expression on her face, she ran through the interview with Noah in her head. She had been sure he was going to crack at the end. She had forced him to actually think about what had happened while he was with Simpson. She had hoped it would be enough, but apparently it had not been.

Turning a corner, she ran into James Larsen, who had been visiting his injured teammates. "So, how did it go?" he asked. "With Noah, I mean."

"I've rattled him, but it didn't do me any good," she answered crisply. "If this doesn't work, Larsen, I am going to have no choice but to remove him from duty." Her eyes told him how reluctant she was to see that happen, and Larsen was one of the few people outside the organization who understood what it really meant.

Larsen sucked in his cheeks. "And will you survive if you have to do that?"

She didn't answer, but only stared at him.

———

THE NIGHT BEFORE, knowing that Allison was preparing for battle, Derek Simpson had made his way through the maze of hospital corridors with the help of his newly acquired asset, Angie Morrison. He had one purpose in mind: to put a stop to Allison Peterson interfering in his missions and getting rid of Noah. All the bitch had to do was sign off on his report. Everything would go back to normal, and Noah would be just as good as ever at his job.

He knew he had to get to Noah before the director did. He couldn't stop Peterson questioning Noah, but he could make sure the young man knew he wasn't alone and that he still had a friend he could count on and also, most importantly, Derek needed to make sure Noah stuck to the correct version of the events on the Germany assignment.

"I know you did the best you could, kid." Derek's words were laced with understanding; a senior agent explaining the best course of action to a more junior partner who had fouled up. "You didn't set out to get captured, but Peterson—I don't think she sees it that way. You don't need to distract from the job we did by going into details. Reitner got what he deserved and he might as well have blown his own house up."

"Okay." Noah had eventually agreed.

"I knew you would come around," Derek soothed, happy that Noah was finally seeing sense. He looked up at the wall clock, realizing he didn't have much time before the annoyingly attentive nurse he was using as an asset returned.

He kept on at Noah, drilling his version of events into the

younger man's head until there was a soft knock on the door and the insipid blonde nurse slid inside the room.

"Get some sleep, kid. Just remember what I told ya," Derek muttered as he carefully lowered himself back into the wheelchair.

He got no response. Noah's eyes were already closed, his breathing steady.

"Derek, I'm sorry, but we have to go. I'm off duty, if..." Angie Morrison interrupted in a soft whisper.

"I can't tell ya how much this means to me, darlin'." Derek dazzled the young nurse with a toothy smile. His eyes twinkled with false sincerity as he gently stroked his fingers along her arm. "You know, I thought he had died out there." He looked over to the bed and the sleeping figure of the young assassin.

"That's alright, Derek. You men are the real heroes; out there working on your own in the wilderness, trying to make the world a better place." She released the brake to the wheelchair before straightening up. "Let's get you back to your room, you look worn out."

Derek was already blocking out her irritating voice, his thoughts going elsewhere.

What the hell was going on with Noah? When had Noah Wolf turned into such a whiny little girl? "You shouldn't have killed the children, Derek."

Jeez, it's not like we're the damned Red Cross. What did Noah expect? That we'd take a bunch of brats along with us back to Nuremberg?

Derek dropped his head down, doing his best to ignore the mindless chatter of his soon-to-be-deceased asset as she pushed his wheelchair out of the room and into the hallway.

Noah had taken it calmly when they had heard Reitner selling them out to his Russian handler. The young man had become quiet, and on the drive out to Reitner's place, his whole attention had been fixed on checking his weapon time and time again.

"Hey, what's up with you?" he had asked.

"I just want to get this over with, Derek, that's all," Noah had replied as he continued to check over his weapon.

"Yeah, well, put the gun away and cheer up. You'll get to use it soon enough."

When they had arrived, however, Noah seemed to be back to his old self. He took care of Reitner's lackeys without hesitation and had rounded up the traitor's servants without complaint. It was only when Noah had spotted the whole Reitner brood lined up, waiting to help Derek encourage the whining, traitorous bastard Daniel Reitner into filling in the gaps on what intelligence he had passed on to his Russian masters, that he had seen the hesitation in Noah's eyes again.

What the hell was Noah's problem with taking care of business when women and kids were involved? It was a weakness; Derek had gotten past it years ago.

"Oh, Derek, that's one of the men who rescued your friend!" Derek Simpson looked up, a snarl on his face at having his train of thought interrupted.

"I—I—" Angie stuttered at the sudden look of fury twisting the handsome features of her new beau. She pointed down the corridor.

"That man walking toward us, he led the team that rescued your friend." Derek's eyes followed where she pointed and he was instantly on high alert. If he had been armed, James Larsen would have been a dead man.

"Get me out of here. Now!" he snapped. He was not going to face the SEAL at a disadvantage.

"But he rescued your friend," Angie informed him again.

"Be a good girl, darlin'; keep your mouth shut and just do as I tell you." He didn't even acknowledge her huff or the sudden increase in speed of his wheelchair along the corridor. His mind was too busy whirring through the possibilities of this new bit of intel.

Lieutenant Commander James Larsen, hotshot, and a damned pain in the ass do-gooder. If he was the one who rescued

Noah, that explained where the annoying 'Saint Noah' attitude came from.

"Oww!" Derek glanced at the bitch of a nurse who had just smacked his toes into the door on the way in to his room.

"We're here," she sulked.

"Aww, honey pie." Derek smiled up at her; the scowl and anger gone in an instant. "I'm so sorry. I'm just tired and worried about my friend." He patted her hand, resisting the urge to break it.

"That's alright, Derek. You must be exhausted." She suddenly brightened. "Why don't I go make you a nice cup of hot chocolate?"

His jaw clenched and his teeth ground against each other as he struggled to maintain his calm.

Some people just asked to be strangled, cut up into... He brought himself back under control.

"No, thank you, I really just need to get back in bed."

"If you're sure," she said as she pulled back the covers and positioned the wheelchair so he could transfer himself onto the bed. "I mean, I could keep you company, or..." As Derek sat on the edge of the bed, another thought struck. It would be just like that damn hotshot to report his late night visit. He was going to have to act quickly. Once Peterson found out he had gotten to Noah first, she would be out for blood.

Taking his mind off of Allison Peterson momentarily, he turned his attention back to the young nurse, who was carefully removing his slippers, her hands massaging his ankles and feet. She really wasn't his type. He preferred his women to be a bit more worldly wise; preferably a career-minded agency type who understood how the game was played. Each knowing they could take what they wanted from the other and in the morning walk away with no hard feelings.

He knew the little blonde's type all too well. She was so easy to manipulate, it was boring. She wanted the excitement of dating a mysterious, dark and dangerous man. In fact, he was certain the only reason she had joined the military and had become a nurse was so she could find herself some brave, wounded warrior to smother.

He noticed she was smiling up at him and he returned the look, putting his hands on her chin gently in his hand. "Hey, babe, how about you get me a phone? I need to make a call."

For the first time, she looked a little nervous. Dipping her head down, she got to her feet and straightened up her uniform. "They took the phone out. I'm not sure. Ow!"

The yelp came as Derek's hand closed around her wrist lightning fast in a grip akin to that of a predator catching hold of its prey. "Sweetheart, I need to make an urgent call. It could be a matter of life or death."

"But..." Angie winced, clutching at Derek's fingers, which were digging into the soft flesh of her arm.

"C'mon, it's just a phone call." He let go of her wrist, a look of remorse flickering briefly across his features. "But it's very important to me. Please, baby," he cajoled.

"I—all right," she answered softly as she reached into a pocket and took her cell phone out of it. She handed it to him and he noticed that she was trembling.

"Thank you, darlin'. Now, how about you run along and get me something for my pain while I make my call?" He dismissed her with barely a glance.

"Derek, I—I think you owe me an apology."

She was trying to be strong, but Derek could see she was scared.

His eyes narrowed. An apology for what? Ahh... Realization came to him in an instant and he altered his features to show his remorse.

"You're right, I'm sorry. I shouldn't have grabbed you like that, but in my business—well, this call is very important," he emphasized again, taking her hand into his and lifting it to his lips to place a soft kiss to the back of her hand. "I'm very grateful, you know."

She relaxed and he could tell all was forgiven. He waited until she left the room and then dialed a number he knew by heart. When she returned five minutes later, the phone was laying on the bedside table and Derek was wearing a satisfied smirk.

Angie handed him two small pills and a glass of water. "Here and, Derek—you do care about me, right? I mean, you're not just using me?"

"Using you? What makes you think that, darlin'?"

"It's nothing." She sighed. "It's just—well, you never use my —oh, never mind." She watched him take the pills and then took the glass off him.

"Don't worry about a thing, darlin'. Now let me get some sleep, huh, an' I'll see you in the morning."

He waited until she left his room and her footsteps faded away down the hall before opening his hand and studying the two little yellow pills lying in his palm.

Grunting from the effort, he picked up his slippers off the floor and carefully eased open a small hole in the stitching he had made earlier. Sliding the pills inside with two others he had already hidden in the hole, he dropped the slippers back onto the floor. He thought another couple would be enough to give his annoying little asset a nasty heart attack when the time was right.

———

THE SINGLE SQUEAK of a rubber shoe sole on the cheap linoleum flooring was enough to bring Derek from being sound asleep to fully alert. Instantly, he knew he wasn't alone. Turning his head toward the door, he stared straight at a tall, burly young man dressed in a plain black suit and a white shirt.

So the bitch had sent someone to watch him. Larsen must have run straight to the Dragon Lady and this was her response to his late night excursion. Well, she was too late; he just wished he could see her face when she found out.

Using the controls, Derek pressed the button that raised the head of the bed so he could sit up. He studied the guard. This one was military and had some field experience, or maybe just an interesting past. He had a long scar running across his cheek and disappearing into his close cropped hair just above his ear. The wound looked recent and probably had put a temporary stop to a career in covert ops, reducing him to guard duties.

"Good morning, son." Derek grinned at the man. "You got a name?" As expected, he got no reply.

"You keep up that attitude, sonny, and I won't let you order any breakfast." He smirked as the man continued to ignore him.

Derek didn't know that Director Peterson was at this moment preparing herself to grill the young assassin to within an inch of his life, but even if he had known, it wouldn't have mattered. He had already ensured the conversation would go precisely the way he wanted. He didn't have a single doubt that his kid would do anything other than exactly what he'd told him to.

It was several boring hours later when Derek was taken for an MRI scan. The doctor had explained that an earlier x-ray had proven that all the bullet fragments had been successfully removed from his wounds, but now they wanted to check for any other damage that might have been caused.

Somehow, his little nurse accomplice had managed to get the job of taking him to the MRI suite. She waited while he lay, letting the machine whir, bang and crash about him and then had helped him back into the wheelchair. She fussed about, making sure his feet were safely on the rests and then leaned over to tuck a blanket around him.

"Leave it. I'm fine," he grumbled. He was fairly certain she had used up her usefulness.

"I thought I'd take the long way back to your room," she announced, pushing the chair out of the room and into the hallway. "It'll give us some time to talk. I wanted..."

He shut out her words, turning his thoughts to how he was going to get her to take the six tiny little pills he had stashed in his slipper. The MRI procedure, along with her incessant over-attentiveness, was beginning to give him a severe headache.

Suddenly, all thoughts of poisoning cleared away as they rounded a corner and Derek found himself face to face with the duo who had managed to make themselves a serious pain in his backside of late. James Larsen and Allison Peterson stood directly in his path and there was no tactical retreat possible.

For a moment, they just stared at each other. Then Derek's eyes narrowed.

If he couldn't retreat, he'd opt for a full frontal assault. *The best defense is a good offense and I can be pretty damned offensive.*

He continued to smile broadly, directing the full weight of his insincere charms at the duo who warily stared back at him. He noted that Peterson held a clipboard clutched tightly in her right hand. At the same moment, he realized they were just a few doors away from his kid's room.

ELEVEN

"Well, well, if it isn't the hotshot and the Dragon Lady. Don't you two make a nice couple? How was the meeting?"

He could tell by her posture alone that Noah must have stuck to the script. His satisfied grin nearly split his face in two.

The look that passed between the two of them in response to the jibe and the way they moved slightly further apart set something off in Derek's finely tuned perception. There was more to Allison Peterson and James Larsen than just colleagues in arms.

In arms, huh?

He had a momentary memory flash, a little snippet he'd picked up a while back when Peterson was complaining about some of his reports and forgotten about until now. Larsen's name had been in her file as an emergency contact. His broad, insincere smile slowly changed into a knowing leer.

She had been leaning in toward Larsen, just a small shift in her body language easily over-looked, but taken together with the way Larsen's hand had been drifting toward the Station Chief's waist, it meant something more.

"Well, maybe meeting isn't the right word. You should be careful, Larsen. You'll end up getting frostbite in places you won't want to have to explain if you spend time trying to warm up the Dragon Lady."

"Derek," Larsen growled low in warning.

"Oh, I think I hit a nerve." He chuckled. This was better than he could have hoped for. "I bet that's not all that gets hit when you two get together." He turned his gaze toward Allison, his eyes racking up and down her body. "You know, honey, I've always had you figured for the whips and chains type behind closed doors."

"That's enough!" Larsen snapped back angrily. Taking a step forward, he grabbed a handful of Derek's hospital gown while Angie gasped and took an involuntary step backwards. The SEAL had fire in his eyes, his mouth twisted in a snarl.

"Larsen," Allison cautioned. Although she was accustomed to Derek's insults, this was farther than he had ever dared go before. Just another indicator of how far out of control the man had become. Still, starting a fist fight in the hospital was only going to play straight into Derek's hands.

"Go for it, Larsen," Derek challenged. "Or would you rather I be standing before you start swinging?"

Larsen released his hold and stepped back. "Count on it. The next time I see you standing, I'm going to put you on your murderous ass."

"Agent Simpson," Allison began, moving smoothly past Larsen, her eyes locked on Derek. "I think I need to speak to your physician regarding your medication, or is this latest outburst your way of requesting a full profile review?"

Angie made the mistake of letting her hand drift to Derek's shoulder, subconsciously sneaking comfort from the aggressively charged atmosphere surrounding the three people before her. Allison picked up on the movement instantly, turning her full attention on the other woman.

The young nurse gulped as hard, blue eyes stared back at her before fixing on the way her hand was resting on her patient's shoulder.

"You'll need to come by my office, along with your supervisor, when you get done escorting Agent Simpson back to his room," Ms. Peterson informed her coldly.

Derek couldn't have been happier. This was just getting better and better. *Let the Dragon Lady make herself useful and get Nurse what'shername out of my hair.* He relaxed back in the wheelchair, directing his gaze toward Larsen.

"If Noah ever needs a wet nurse again, I'll call you, Larsen." Watching the SEAL stiffen in anger, Derek deliberately turned his mocking gaze back to Allison. "I don't think you'd qualify, my dear. Oh, and you might want to check your messages, sweetheart, before you decide to have another conversation about me with Noah."

Larsen and Allison exchanged glances without looking directly at one another, a skill developed from their time together in the Navy, but Simpson caught it nonetheless.

"Run along now." Derek dismissed them as Angie started to slowly reverse down the hall with the wheelchair. "Nothing going on here that you two need to concern yourselves with anyway." He smirked as the chair was spun around and he was hurried away.

Larsen and Allison silently watched as Angie spun the wheelchair about and pushed it rapidly along the hall toward Derek's room.

"Well, Derek's certainly feeling better," Larsen remarked at length. "Must be all that bathing in blood that does it for him."

"Really, Larsen? That's all you've got to say? Something is seriously wrong if he's feeling brave enough to openly antagonize the both of us that way."

"Ooh, I'm far from happy, Allie. I'll go push the sick son of a bitch under a truck if it will make you feel better."

She shook her head. As tempting as the offer was, she knew it wouldn't end the mess Derek had created.

"I think you should go and prepare for that meeting with

your commander." She looked at her watch. "It's set for seventeen hundred, isn't it?"

"Yeah," he said, "but it's not that late already, is it?" Larsen rubbed at his chin, his eyes still fixed on the direction Derek had been pushed away by the wide-eyed nurse.

"No, but you need to go for a walk and calm down a bit before the debrief and I need to go..." Derek's comment about checking her messages suddenly rang in her head and she knew in an instant what had happened. "Damn! That nurse must have gotten him a phone. She is done!" she ground out between clenched teeth, her jaw set and her blue eyes blazing.

"Hey, hey, go easy on her, Allie. It's like I told you before, Derek's a force to be reckoned with and that girl has to be crazy, because she looked absolutely in love."

"Well, her little love affair just ended her career," she replied flatly. "Come see me before you go to turn up the heat on Noah."

———

TWO HOURS LATER, Allison Peterson was pacing her office floor, her fingers tightly pinching the bridge of her nose. She had been right; that son of a bitch had managed to get a call out, and as if Derek's contact knew her movements, he had been waiting on the line when she had walked back into her office. It was the same asshole who had drawn her and Noah into this mess.

Why hadn't she handed in the mission reports on Simpson's Germany assignment? Didn't she realize the political implications of her dilly-dallying? Had she thought about how it looked to their new German allies that she was delaying closure on the case?

Then the veiled threats had come: did she like her job? Maybe E&E was too much for her to handle. Was she admitting that she had lost control of her agents?

And finally the part of the conversation that had made her want to hurl the phone across the room.

If she was serious about her career and she ever wanted another promotion, she had better learn how to look at the big picture. Simpson and Noah had turned out to be a successful team. They had done a good job exposing Daniel Reitner. The oversight committee was considering moving Noah to CIA for that reason.

When the call ended, she had carefully placed the handset back on its cradle and slumped back in her chair.

The sorry bastard had done it again.

"Oh, and you might want to check your messages, sweetheart, before you decide to have another conversation with Noah."

A vision of Derek Simpson's smug, smiling face danced before Allison Peterson's eyes as she paced back and forth, wearing a hole in the linoleum covering the floor of her temporary office at Sigonella. Not only had Simpson blind-sided her for a second time in less than a year, he had done it in such a way that her hands were now completely tied.

Two hours after one of the most unpleasant conversations she'd had to endure in quite a while, she was no further along in finding a solution to her 'Derek problem.' Eventually she slumped down in her chair, her elbows resting on the desktop, her hands on either side of her head. She could still hear that voice coming through the phone line.

"Ms. Peterson, I'm so pleased to get a hold of you. I do confess I'm a bit annoyed about the delay in your releasing that final report on Agent Simpson's Germany assignment. Are you aware of the political implications of your hesitation? I'm sure it was just an oversight on your part, although I have always wondered if perhaps such a prestigious position as director of your agency could've been too much responsibility for a wo—for somebody only on their first posting to such an office."

She had picked up on his near slip. The CIA Director was a renowned womanizer who made Derek Simpson sound like an advocate for women's rights. She had only met him face to face once and that had been enough. He had held her hand a little too long and throughout the meeting had made his interest plain.

"I have to ask, are you serious about your career? It seems like I've had to remind you to look at the big picture before. Agents Simpson and Noah make a very effective team. I've put in a request to have Wolf transferred to CIA to keep them together, and it's being considered."

Grateful? Grateful for having to find a way of controlling an agent who was apparently a covert homicidal maniac, and taking away the best assassin she'd ever found? She studied the folder laying before her, flipping open the thin cardboard cover of Derek Simpson's mission debrief. She stared at the neatly printed words covering the page. This was what she was expected to sign off on? Slamming the folder closed, she pushed it away from herself in disgust.

That work of fiction was only part of the problem and the other part—she couldn't even bring herself to ask Logan to pull out the necessary paperwork.

The final part of the conversation had made her want to hurl the phone across the room. Instead, she had gritted her teeth and promised to look up that 'missing' report and make sure it reached his office in D.C. at the earliest opportunity.

Dragging the folder back in front of her, she opened it again. Taking a deep breath to prepare herself, she began to read Derek's version of events as dictated to Agent Logan. She was halfway down the second page when she was interrupted by a knock on her door.

"Enter," she called out, closing the folder.

James Larsen paused in the doorway, his brown eyes registering concern when he noted the stress lines on her face.

"Problems?" he asked.

"You have no idea. Come in and shut the door," she answered softly, her voice flat and the look in her eyes anything but friendly.

By the time Larsen turned back around from shutting the door, Allison was on her feet, her mouth set in a hard, thin line and her arms crossed over her chest.

"It seems Simpson was very busy last night. Not only did he

manage to get in to see Noah and make sure he learned all his lines, he also found time to get a call out to D.C. I've just had a very interesting conversation with Alex Walker."

Larsen winced. "As in the man in charge of the CIA?"

"The very same," she finished his sentence. "And he wants— no, he has as good as ordered me to close down the investigation on what happened in Germany. He's even trying to get Noah transferred to CIA to work full time with Derek Simpson."

"Holy shit." Larsen whistled through his teeth.

"Oh, you haven't heard the best part yet." Her usual calm, controlled demeanor was slipping away before his eyes. "That murderous bastard is to be rewarded for his actions. He and Noah both are supposed to be awarded commendations and I have to put my name on that recommendation."

"What the hell?" Larsen snapped in disbelief, his eyes following her as she moved from behind the desk to pace about the room.

"Apparently it'll let those brave boys know just how much the folks back home appreciate their sacrifices." She did a passable impersonation of Walker.

"Ouch!" Larsen winced, taking a step back as she shot him a look filled with venom.

"This is partially your fault, you and your 'go easy on Noah.' I should have come down hard on him as soon as he regained consciousness and maybe even burned him right then. I had everything I needed." She shook her head in disgust. "But now? Once Walker approves those commendations, my hands will be tied."

She came to a stop in front of him, pointing to the folder still laying on the desk. "I can hold off sending out that work of fiction for maybe twenty-four hours at best. In the meantime..." She stabbed him in the middle of his broad chest with a rigid finger. "I want you to get to work on Noah. I want you to make it absolutely clear that I'm done with him and that I've got all the paperwork ready for him to be sent over to Langley. Make him believe he has just one chance to tell me the whole truth about what happened on that mission."

Larsen sucked in a deep breath as he realized her plan. "Allison, don't—"

"Larsen." She stared back at him, her expression deadly serious. "I have to stop them and it's not like I have the luxury of time any more. Once Walker approves those commendations, any hope I had of burning Noah or saving him will be gone." She leaned back against the desk. "I'm sorry. I know you like Noah. I think of him like one of my own kids, for God's sake. Before he was teamed up with Simpson, he was one of my best assets." Allison held up a hand, as Larsen was already shaking his head negatively. "Look, you've seen it for yourself. With Noah on his side, Simpson is getting more and more brazen and out of control. I can't touch Derek, but I can and I will shut Noah down if that's what it takes to stop this, even if it costs me my job."

"Don't do this, Allie. You know it's wrong. Railroading Noah, it's a low trick." Larsen closed the gap between them, gently putting his hands on her shoulders and staring into her eyes. "Why can't you send him back to Neverland? That head injury would be a legitimate reason to break up their team while he recovers, and maybe he'll get his head out of his ass. I understand he has some sort of twisted loyalty to Simpson, but I'm telling you, he isn't a monster, at least not yet. Give him some time and some room to think things through and he'll come around."

She shook her head, a look of determination on her face. "He's already had more chances than he deserved. Hell, he's been rogue more than once, but at least the other times it was to save my ass or the country. If he lets Simpson get away with this, then he's gone too far this time."

Before Larsen could speak again, the telephone on Allison's desk began to ring. She held up an index finger before reaching across and picking up the handset and listening to someone on the other end of the line.

"Ask them to wait. I'll be finished here in a minute." She placed the handset back on the desk.

"Captain Dickerson and Derek's latest conquest are waiting in the other room. I have to deal with that young lady now. Go speak to Noah." She paused, reading the indecision in his eyes. "Look, you'll be doing him a favor. If he keeps on working with Derek, you said it yourself, he'll become a monster. If you can get him to roll on Simpson, there's a chance I can keep him at E&E."

Larsen nodded and turned away. "Okay, okay, I'll speak to him, but just give it a bit more thought, please."

Larsen left Allison's office, nodding to Logan, who was still sitting at his desk before glancing over to where a stony-faced, dark-haired woman dressed in fatigues which displayed the rank of a captain sat next to Derek's blonde-haired nurse. The younger woman glanced up at him, her face set in a scowl.

Leaving the office, Larsen felt a small amount of pity for the young, impressionable nurse. Allison Peterson was definitely out for the blood of the person who let Derek Simpson get his hands on a phone.

As he walked along the maze of corridors, Larsen tried to work out the best strategy for getting Noah Wolf's cooperation. He knew without a doubt that trying to trick the younger man into revealing what had happened inside Reitner's farmhouse would not work.

Besides, he'd always preferred the straightforward approach.

TWELVE

Exhausted after his less than friendly conversation with Director Peterson, Noah had fallen into a deep sleep, so deep that he barely stirred when a nurse came in to clean and re-dress his head wound and replace the IV bags filled with saline, antibiotics and pain relief medication. Outwardly he looked at peace, but looks were deceiving. Inside, his morale was taking a beating from all sides.

"If Derek gets away with what he's done this time, what's he going to ask you to cover up next?" James Larsen's voice echoed through Noah's head.

"You won't be held responsible for what he did if you step up, Noah. It's the right thing to do." So calm, so reasonable, sounding so disgusted that he was having to explain something that any decent human being would know without having to be told.

But Larsen didn't understand; how could he? He didn't know about all of the bodies already stacked up behind him. There were so many, too many to count. There were the ones who had deserved it. Others who were simply in the wrong place at the wrong time, and then there were those who should have run away screaming as soon as he had come into view. He had lost count. Was it wrong that he had stopped counting?

What else could Derek ask him to do that he hadn't done already? Destroy a man's reputation, ruin another's life? Done and done. Manipulate, threaten, blackmail an asset? Not a problem. Interrogate, torture? If it gets the job done. Kill? That was his speciality, and it was intended to stop other deaths.

The children, Derek, why did you kill the children? If he could just find a way of blocking out the image of that lone stuffed toy, he might get past this. *"What did you want to do with them, kid? Take them with us? I know, you could open an orphanage, Saint Noah's home for lost causes. No? Well, stop acting like some liberal asshole. We both know it isn't you."*

The scene replayed in his mind, but this time it was his hand on the gun. He could feel the welcoming sensation of the checkered hand grip against his palm, his finger curling around the trigger, knowing a light squeeze would end the life of one of the thirteen pieces of leverage bound and gagged before him. It was his voice demanding answers from the terrified man at his feet, who was begging him to stop what he was doing.

The jolt of the recoil barely registered, the sound of another lifeless body hitting the floor left him unmoved, the cries of the man begging for mercy meant nothing.

The broken bodies of men, women and children lay dead around him as blood pooled about his feet.

Derek was wrong. He didn't feel alive. He felt—numb.

Noah's eyes fluttered open, a wave of nausea sending his hand out, blindly reaching for one of the bowls an orderly had left beside his bed. Gagging and coughing, he got the bowl up to his chin just in time.

Afterward, he slowly pulled himself into a sitting position. His stomach was still turning somersaults and his head throbbed so badly he wanted to pass out. Whimpering from the pain and the memory of his blood filled nightmare, he wrapped his arms around his own trembling body.

"I didn't do anything," he muttered quietly, desperately trying to soothe himself. If he kept telling himself that, then maybe he could make himself believe it.

"The civilian casualty rate just keeps going up when Derek is around, doesn't it?" He closed his eyes.

"I've never killed a man who didn't deserve it."

"You couldn't subdue two civilians? But you took apart a highly trained, six man Spetsnaz team?" Peterson raised an eyebrow, doubt written across her stern features.

He gasped, opening his eyes again to look around. He could have sworn that she was there in the room with him, but he was alone. The guard was standing out in the hall. He could see his shadow through the frosted glass on the door.

The two civilians... had the two men patrolling outside Reitner's farmhouse deserved to die? He hadn't even considered knocking them out and tying them up.

He reached out with a shaking hand for the glass of water sitting on top of the bedside table. Sipping the cool liquid, he tried to focus his thoughts. The drink didn't help and his heart began to pound as he came to a sickening realization. Reitner's sentries both had had shotguns slung across their backs, but neither had accessed their weapons when he had pounced.

"Sometimes there's collateral damage on a mission. Don't worry about it, kid. You have to weigh up the costs. You've got to look at the big picture."

"I've never killed a man who didn't deserve it," he repeated firmly.

"Finally, you're getting it. You're no hotshot, Noah. You never were."

In a flush of unfamiliar anger, he flung the glass across the room and flinched when it hit the wall and shattered, scattering slivers of glass over the floor. He remained unmoving when the guard came into the room, his jacket open and his hand on his gun.

The man looked around the room and then stared pointedly

at the watery mess on the floor before turning his gaze to Noah, sitting up on the bed.

"It fell," Noah answered the man's stare.

It had to be the drugs they had given him. He couldn't think clearly. Things would be better once he was out of the hospital and back on his feet. He had too much time to think about the past when he should be concentrating on his future.

"As soon as the medical team here gives you an all clear, I intend to call you in for a full performance review and psych evaluation. This time, Agent Simpson will not be present to hold your hand."

He wasn't worried about the review or the psych evaluation. He had been through one before.

"I've got your back, kid. I've got the connections to keep you safe. All you have to do is stick by me. I'll get us commendations for this. After all, we're heroes. We just exposed a Russian spy to the German government."

He watched as an orderly came into the room to clear away the mess he had made. The whole time, the guard stood on full alert. He was alone, but not abandoned. He just had to hold his nerve until Derek came through on his promise.

Partners look out for one another, they cover each other's backs. It wasn't the only reason why he would keep quiet. It was his upbringing, too. Since childhood, there was one rule that was never broken, one rule not even his father at his most drunk or vicious had ever been willing to break: you don't rat out your family or friends.

Wiping a hand wearily over his eyes, he let his head gently fall back onto the pillows. If he held his nerve and Derek got him out of whatever trouble Allison was planning to drop on him, then what? This act of Derek's was likely to bind them together permanently. If that happened, he wondered what would become of Team Camelot.

The team. He wondered what they were thinking about all of this.

"Hmmm, it's always amazed me what some people will do when they think they have no choice." Director Peterson continued to mock him, her eyes full of disdain. Or was it... pity?

What else could he do? What other choice did he have? He would not talk about what happened in that farmhouse. He was never going to talk about it. Nothing happened, but he also knew he had used up any good will Allison had left for him. She would never take him back into the fold after this, it was too great a betrayal.

"You never did listen, Noah, not to me or anyone. Now see where your stubbornness has gotten you." He groaned and rolled onto his side, the smell of tobacco and stale liquor filling his nostrils, the sanctimonious whining tones of his father invading his mind. He could not go back home. He had to figure out some way of keeping his job.

"I didn't do anything," he muttered as fatigue took over his mind and body, sending him back to his nightmares.

———

"Sir, you can't go in there."

Noah forced his eyelids to open. That was the Dragon Lady's guard. He felt his heart lift. It had to be Derek coming in to tell him it was over. One of his contacts in D.C. must have come through. It was going to be okay, it was. So, why wasn't he happy about it? Another unfamiliar emotion crept in; a faint glimmer of despair. Where was that coming from?

He closed his eyes for a second. He had to pull himself together. The indecision he was feeling was going to end up getting him killed, burned or maybe thrown in prison. He hardened his resolve. He had no choice. He needed the job, the way of life; there was no way he was going to be sent home. He had joined the military to avoid going to jail. Besides that, he had spent the last eight years in either the army or E&E. He knew no other way to live.

"I still can't let you enter, sir."

He strained to hear what was going on outside his door as the guard repeated the order.

"I have permission from Director Peterson. Call her."

It was Larsen. Noah closed his eyes. This was going to be another uncomfortable visit with the SEAL commander.

Moments later, the door opened and the SEAL strolled inside.

"Hey, Noah, you feeling any better?" Larsen inquired as he got a chair from the corner of the room.

"Yeah." He gave a weary smile. "I'm getting better all the time."

"That's good," Larsen answered, still trying to work out the best way of getting the answers Allison wanted.

They remained silent for a moment. Noah could only think of what was happening outside his room. Had Derek done any good? Was Peterson backing down, or had the Dragon Lady beaten Derek at his own game?

In the end, he could take no more. "Why are you here, Larsen? I mean, I thought I was under arrest or something."

Larsen pursed his lips, his eyes hardened. "Okay, buddy, I've been trying to think of the best way to do this, but it's like you've already told me maybe a half dozen times, I'm not an assassin, I won't get it, so I'm just gonna come out and tell you the truth; your pal Derek has managed to pull strings again. He got you both off."

Noah felt a weight lift. He let out a long sigh and couldn't help the smile that lit up his pale, drawn features. He was so wrapped up in his own feeling of relief that he didn't even notice Larsen's look of utter disgust.

"Oh, but that's not all. He talked his pals back in D.C. into handing you both medals for the great job you did. Doesn't that make you feel proud?" Larsen added.

"A medal?" That set Noah back, confusion showing on his face.

They had done nothing that merited a medal. Suddenly, he felt sick as Derek's words came back to haunt him.

"I'll get us commendations for this; after all, we're heroes. We just exposed a Russian spy to the German government."

"Yeah, kid, a medal for murdering a room full of women and children. How's that make you feel?"

"I..." Noah couldn't speak.

A medal? He didn't want a medal, they had done nothing, he had done nothing.

He was going to be sick. His vision swam as all he could see were dead bodies piled up in the corner of the old, rustic kitchen. The stench of death filled his nostrils and his mouth. He was losing himself in the vivid flashback.

The thought of somebody rewarding them both for that evening's work sickened him. He suddenly felt completely alone as the true horror of his situation hit. He was going to have to stand up, accept a medal and smile.

Larsen studied the younger man's face. Noah lay on the bed looking pale, his pinched features expressionless, his eyes unfocused. Larsen couldn't decide if his words were having an effect, or if Noah was just ignoring him.

"Hey, let me tell you something, Noah. If you can lay there and accept a reward for committing murder, you're no different than that soulless monster, Simpson. I thought you were better than that." He got to his feet and flung the chair back across the room. "I wash my hands of you."

Larsen's heart sank when he got no response. He had been wrong all along. It was as if the Noah Wolf he knew had died, leaving a doppelganger in his place.

It was the crash of the chair hitting the opposite wall that pulled Noah back to the present; he had barely heard Larsen's words as the pounding of his heart blocked out all other noise.

Panic had sent his heart rate rocketing; he couldn't do it. He couldn't let them pin a medal on his chest for what happened.

He stared wildly about the room, his eyes fixing on Larsen's back as he walked through the doorway.

"Larsen!" He needed help, he had absolutely no idea what to do. "Larsen, wait!" The door slammed shut and Noah was completely alone. He listened to the sound of boots marching away from him down the corridor and his world came crashing down around him as the protective wall he had built up over the years cracked and began to crumble.

"I'm sorry." His voice was barely more than a whisper. "I..." He brought his hands up to his eyes, trying to halt the moisture that was beginning to flow. He had absolutely no idea what to do next, and the one person left who might have helped him had just walked out the door.

———

LARSEN STORMED out of the room, letting the door slam shut behind him. Ignoring the startled look on the guard's face, he strode away without a backward glance. As he made his way back toward Allison's office, Larsen ran through what had just occurred. How could he have misread Noah Wolf's character so badly? He had really believed Noah would step up and admit what had happened in that German farmhouse. Instead, the young spy had just stared up at the ceiling as if the words meant nothing to him.

Larsen suddenly came to a stop. When he had stormed out of Noah's room, he had been angry, not just with the younger man, but with himself too, but now with a slightly clearer head, the memory of Noah's blank, staring expression had him worried. He had thought Noah was ignoring him, but what if he had been wrong?

"Shit!" He turned on his heel, rushing back the way he had just came.

THIRTEEN

THE SHARP SLAM OF THE DOOR, FOLLOWED BY ECHOING footfalls fading into the distance, and he was alone.

"I'm sorry!" But he knew it was too little, too late. He had driven away the last person who might have helped him.

"I'm sorry," he repeated as his world crumbled. "I..." Blackness enveloped him, dragging him into despair. It was as if he was back in the pit James Larsen had pulled him out of four days ago.

With all his defenses stripped away, Noah Wolf caved in. Collapsing back onto the hospital bed, he curled into a protective ball, his knees drawn up close to his chest and his arms wrapped tightly around his torso.

Great, gulping breaths hitched in his throat, struggling free in heart wrenching sobs. He wanted it all to stop, all the pain and the torment, all the having to hold everything inside while maintaining the illusion of unshakable confidence.

The flood of raw emotions unleashed by James Larsen's blunt announcement and brutal honesty in telling him how Derek had prevailed had floored him in every sense. He could finally see it all clearly, every act he had witnessed or committed in the last three years. Not only the people he and his team had killed, but the lives they destroyed without a thought.

A successful team, they were, a team who got the job done at any cost.

It was what he had wanted, it defined him. All the time he'd been with E&E, his emotionless nature making him the best Allison had, it had been all he wanted.

"I don't want it anymore."

They were the team that was called up when there was a dirty job to be done, and they took on all the dirty jobs and did the work without hesitation, jobs that nobody else wanted or had the ability to do.

"I can't do it, I won't."

"If we work together, we can be unstoppable," Derek had told him. *"We're a damned effective team. We can do what we like as long as the job gets done."*

"No! Not anymore. I won't accept a medal for what we did. It has to stop now."

The cold truth came through at last: Derek Simpson had to be stopped.

He sniffed and furiously wiped at his eyes. As his heart hammered away in his chest, a strange calm settled over him. There was no way out of his situation; he had dug himself into a hole following Derek's lead. There was nobody left to help him out. He couldn't quit and he was nothing without the job. He couldn't do what Peterson wanted and he was pretty sure he couldn't continue doing what Derek wanted either.

"Noah?"

Pressing the heels of his hands against his eyes, Noah tried to block out the terrible conclusion his mixed-up mind had come up with. Another choking sob rose up in his throat and tremors shot through his body.

"Noah, you okay in there, buddy?"

This was far worse than the pit. In that deep, dark hole, he had been fighting to escape and had been determined to survive. Now, all he wanted was the darkness and the peace and the deathly silence.

"Noah, it's Larsen. I'm gonna come in, okay?"

"Larsen?" Noah gulped, sniffed and wiped at his face. "No—I—yeah, come in."

———

LARSEN STOOD outside Noah Wolf's room, pressing his forehead against the door as he listened intently to the sounds of despair coming from inside the room. The muffled, drawn out, wheezing sobs were the only confirmation he needed that he had been right to come rushing back. Taking a deep breath, he knocked lightly on the door's frosted glass panel.

"Noah?" He spoke in a low, quiet tone, not wanting to spook the young man on the other side. The sounds of somebody at the end of their rope had ended, but he got no answer to his call.

"What did you do in there?" The guard shot him an accusing glance. "I should report this."

"Give it a rest, okay?" Larsen muttered, dismissing the guard's concerns with a wave of his hand before calling out again. "Noah? You okay in there, buddy?" He really didn't want to just burst through the door, but if he didn't get an answer soon, that was precisely what he was going to have to do. The sounds of utter despair started up again. Dropping his head down, Larsen closed his eyes and took a moment to prepare himself before entering the room.

"Noah," he called out clearly, "it's Larsen. I'm gonna come in, okay?" He gripped the door handle, pushing down to release the catch, when the choking sobs stopped again.

"Larsen?" He barely recognized Noah's voice. "No—I—yeah, come in." Noah's stammered reply sounded so defeated that Larsen wasn't sure what he was going to find when he went through the door. He gave the younger man another couple of seconds to pull himself together before he stepped into the room.

Noah was laying on his side almost in a fetal position with his back to him. Closing the door quietly, Larsen stepped further into the room.

"Noah?"

He rubbed a hand over his jaw, a little dismayed when Noah remained mute, not even acknowledging his presence. Since when did anybody who worked in covert ops put their back to a door and not even glance around when somebody was behind them? Noah had to be in an even worse state than he had first thought.

"I'm just gonna get something to sit on and then we can talk." Crossing the room, Larsen recovered the chair he had abandoned earlier and set it down facing the younger man. Up close, he could see the full effects of his earlier visit and it gave him a faint glimmer of hope that there was still something left of the Noah Wolf he used to know.

"So, are you ready to come to your senses?" He kept his eyes focused on the top rail of the headboard above Noah's head, not wanting to look directly at the younger man's shattered expression and red-rimmed eyes.

Noah sniffed again and turned to lay on his back, grimacing at the pain the movement caused. He twisted his head as far in the opposite direction as he could while scrubbing his hands vigorously over his face, doing all he could to hide the signs of his breakdown from the SEAL.

Larsen let out a sigh. He really wanted to help, but he needed Noah to at least show he was willing to accept that help. If he wouldn't even speak...

"Noah, I want to help you, I really do, but you need to talk to me, buddy."

"I can't," came the mumbled reply.

"Then there's nothing I can do for you. Sorry, kid." Larsen got slowly to his feet, the chair scraping noisily against the floor.

"Don't go."

The plea was spoken so quietly, the voice so broken, it caused Larsen to sit back down. "I won't leave, as long as you tell me you've come to your senses." He pushed for an answer.

Noah shuddered and scrubbed at his face once more before finally shifting in the bed until he was facing Larsen. "That m-medal. I can't t-take it," he stammered.

"If you don't want it, refuse to accept it. You know what you have to do, Noah. It's not rocket science. Come clean to Peterson about what that psychopath did to those people in Germany."

He stared at the look of horror that flickered over the younger man's face as he began to babble.

"No, no, no." Noah tried to shake his head, but pain from his head wound forced him to stop. "Nothing happened. I didn't do anything. I couldn't stop it—no, no, no. I wasn't even there." He pressed his fists into his eyes as if to block out everything around him.

"Okay, okay." Larsen leaned forward, gently gripping Noah's arm in an effort to calm him down and to stop him from turning away again. "Listen, Noah, stop thinking you're the only one who's gone through this sorta thing. We all make mistakes; it's how we deal with them that counts."

"I can't talk about it. Nothing happened," Noah mumbled stubbornly.

Larsen shifted uneasily in his chair, not liking the strange mix of defiance and desperation creeping into the younger man's tone.

"Well, I dunno what I can do for you if you're not willing to even try to help yourself." He let go of Noah's arm and moved his chair back. There were limits to even his patience, and Noah Wolf was pushing him rapidly toward them.

"Please. I—please, Larsen, I need this job. I have nothing else." Noah clutched desperately at Larsen's arm, his fear of being left to cope on his own as he drowned in a sea of conflicting emotions driving him to reach out.

Larsen paused as that one sentence transported him back ten years and to a muddy field in east Germany, to the time he had made the biggest screw up of his whole life. He wondered if he had looked quite so desperate and lonely when he had pleaded with the only man who could save him.

They were huddled down in a water and slime filled ditch, shaking from the exertion of evading an east German border patrol for three hours. The reason for their present state? He had fouled up on a massive scale. Larsen remembered how scared he had been and filled with remorse for what he had done. A dumb, stupid, thoughtless mistake, which could have cost a lot of lives, if it hadn't been for the man at his side.

"Jack, I need this job. I have nothing else." He had sounded just like Noah and had probably worn the same desperate expression. He'd used exactly the same words, and he was forever grateful for what Jack had said next.

"You're not a SEAL, Larsen, you're a screwup." Jack had growled at him, wiping away the water that was dripping into his eyes. "You really messed up on this one. This is beyond FUBAR, but since no one's died, I'm gonna polish this turd for you and keep my mouth shut an' you're gonna do the same. Everyone deserves a second chance. Just remember that this is your one and only, Larsen. You do anything like that again and you'll be up in front of the mast so fast your boots won't touch the ground and I'll shred your ass myself. Got it?"

"I got it, Jack, I'm—"

"What part of 'keep your mouth shut' didn't you understand, sailor?"

Larsen sucked in a breath, his hand unconsciously going to his SEAL badge as he remembered Jack's threat. Jack had never mentioned the incident again, not even a single reference regarding his mistake. Okay, he hadn't just killed a roomful of helpless civilians, but a lot of people could have died because of what he did. He had been lucky, and if it hadn't been for Jack...

In a way, Larsen thought he could understand Noah's loyalty to a friend, even if that friend was a twisted psychopath. It was obvious Noah was not going to talk, but sending him back to Derek or burning him was not the right answer.

"Noah, I'll do what I can for you, but I want your word you're done with Derek Simpson. No matter what, you gotta promise me you won't have anything to do with him again. Can you do that?"

He watched Noah's expression carefully. Noah was an assassin. His whole career was based around lying and telling people what they wanted to hear.

For the first time since he had come back into the room, Larsen got a full look at Noah's features as Noah stared back at him. His expression was solemn and there was a hint of fear in his eyes.

"Okay, I'll do it," he replied in a firm, soft tone.

"I mean it, Noah, I'm gonna do my best to talk your boss into a deal. Maybe get you sent home on medical leave for a good long while. It should give you some breathing space while Derek gets reassigned elsewhere, but if you're jerkin' me around..."

He let the threat hang in the air.

"Whatever you want. I want him gone," Noah replied dully.

Larsen got to his feet and patted his arm. "Good man. Try to get some rest now, while I try to sort out a deal for you."

Noah nodded and attempted a smile, but it didn't quite work out for him.

Director Peterson was not going to be easy to convince.

———

LARSEN TOOK A LONG, slow walk back to Allison's office. He needed time to plan an approach and then gather the necessary intel to run the op. He was nothing if not methodical in his strategy. By the time he entered Allison's outer office, he had everything he needed.

Agent Logan was busy dealing with a phone call. From the agitated look on the young man's face, Larsen guessed it had to be something important, so he signaled toward the Station Chief's door and got a nod back, telling him it should be safe to enter. After knocking on the door, he didn't have long to wait for the order to come on in.

It was a shame Logan had been busy. When going in search of favors, Larsen preferred to know exactly the mindset of the person he was going to be asking for help. It made the situation so much easier to work with.

He found Allison Peterson sitting at her desk with her head tipped all the way back while the fingers of her right hand pinched the bridge of her nose. Larsen took a moment to admire the view of her muted green shirt being stretched tight before clearing his throat.

"I take it Derek's latest flame didn't go quietly." He closed the door before sliding into the chair facing her across her desk. "She looked like a handful." He remembered the young woman's scowling expression.

Allison let her head drop back into a more natural position. After blinking her eyes a couple of times to restore her vision to normal, she sighed. "Nurse Morrison wasn't the problem. It was the base's Chief of Nursing, Captain Julia Dickerson. She really isn't a fan of the intelligence services in general and me in particular."

"She give you a hard time, Allie?" Larsen felt his confidence wane. If Allison had just had a bad meeting with the nursing staff, she was going to be even less inclined to help a rogue assassin, however sorry that assassin was feeling.

"Apparently at the time Nurse Morrison took Simpson to visit his colleague, I had not ordered him to be confined to his room, and, although I had requested the phone be removed from his room, I had not issued any order requesting that he was denied outside contact." She pressed her fingers into either side of her temples and squinted at him. "She did, however, concede that Morrison's behavior was unprofessional."

"So what's happening?"

"I've had Simpson moved to a more secure room next to the nursing station and with a camera set up watching the door, so he won't be sneaking out again. Dickerson has promised that Morrison will be disciplined and, during Simpson's stay, she is barred from working on the surgical ward, but basically that idiot nurse who helped cause this mess—my hands are tied. I can't do a damn thing about it," she complained angrily.

Larsen got to his feet. Moving around behind her, he dropped his hands onto her shoulders and began to massage away the tight knots in her sore neck and upper back. "So, not what you wanted?" he consoled.

FOURTEEN

She relaxed under his hands, enjoying the sensation. The whole day had been one colossal screw up. It was late and...

"Larsen, what happened with Noah?" She moved away from his hands and twisted in her chair so she could see him clearly.

"Well..." He took a step back.

Allison's eyes narrowed as she realized what he had been doing, trying to get her to relax and maybe help her into a better mood before asking for a favor.

"Larsen, just get it over with, what happened?"

"Noah isn't going to talk," he announced bluntly. It was like ripping off a dressing. Get the bad news over and out of the way in one swift move and then you can move on to fixing the problem.

"So Simpson wins."

"No, no, you can still salvage at least some of the situation. Noah is really broken up. He's finally realized what they did and he wants out."

"Oh, he's out alright," she agreed, back on her feet now. "I'll get the paperwork done tonight."

"Hey, hey, you didn't let me finish." Larsen covered her hand as she reached for the phone.

"There is nothing to say. I asked you to talk him into giving up Simpson. You just said he isn't going to do it, so that's the end of the matter."

"Noah was your best, Allie. You need to salvage this man, or he'll be dead within weeks."

This made her pause. She studied Larsen's expression. "You're serious?"

"He swore to me that he wants nothing more to do with Derek Simpson."

Deflated, Allison sat back down. "I don't know if he can be salvaged. He was the best because of his lack of emotion, but his medical charts say that may be over." She sighed. "The base shrink says the head trauma may have overridden the trauma that caused his condition when he was a kid, so all the emotions he kept bottled up inside all these years could come out all at once. We've worried a couple times before that it was happening, but he always pulled himself together. Now, this time? I'm not sure there's any hope of that."

Larsen rubbed at his forehead. "Can't you send Noah back to Neverland and take him out of action for a while? Use his head wound as a reason for extended medical leave, get him into some kind of therapy that might help him get back to where he was?"

"The problem is that where he was happened to be the result of severe emotional trauma when he was only seven. There's no way to put Humpty-Dumpty back together again, if he's fallen apart."

Larsen checked his watch as his stomach began to complain about the lack of attention it had been receiving. "Look, it's late. Let's check in at the chow hall and get something to eat while we review Derek and Noah's medical records." He picked up two folders he had had in his hand when he'd entered the room. "If we can permanently separate the two of them, it would be a start, wouldn't it?"

She gave him a sideways look and then a weary smile. "I know what you're doing, Larsen, and it's not going to work. Noah is no longer going to be as effective as he was."

"Maybe not," Larsen said. "He's had a head injury, Allie. Even the most stable of us can go crazy for a while after that. How do you know he won't recover to be the same guy he was before?"

She stared into his eyes, her lips pursed and her eyes piercing. This was what she both loved and hated about James Larsen, he was so damn persistent and—sneaky. "And you want me to risk everything, including my agency and my career, on that slim hope?"

"Does that mean you'll look at Noah's case again?" he asked hopefully.

"Look, Larsen, that's all. Just look." She drew away from him, keeping eye contact, a small smile playing on her lips.

Before he could stop her, she snatched the folders from his hand and stuck them under her arm. "Food first, I don't intend to discuss Noah or Simpson while I'm eating."

"No talking about Noah or Simpson until after we eat." They walked a bit farther in silence before she spoke again. Larsen didn't reply, he just smiled and kept at her side on the walk across the compound. Allison Peterson could be stubborn, but she also had a strong sense of right and wrong. Given time and a few gentle nudges, he was sure she would do the right thing.

———

TWO HOURS LATER, after a hot meal, they had retired back to her temporary quarters. With the work day finally over, Allison let her hair out of its tight plait and with a sigh, relaxed back against Larsen's chest as he carefully combed his fingers through her shoulder length, dirty blonde hair before he returned to massaging the tension out of her shoulders. As his fingers began to wander lower, she stopped him, laying her own hands over his.

"Allie?" he asked, his breath whispering into her ear, sending a tingle down her spine.

"You wanted to discuss Noah," she reminded him as she led him across the room to a cozy two seater couch. "Come sit down and we'll go through those reports while you try to convince me he's not just trying to get out of being burned."

As he sat, sinking into the deep, soft cushions, he pulled her down next to him.

"Okay." He reached out and grabbed one of the folders. "Let's just suppose you agree to Noah's medical leave and take a look at Derek's report. Hopefully, he's well enough to be sent to some hot spot where he has a decent chance of getting himself killed."

They sat in companionable silence, focusing their attention on the final pages. Finally, Larsen closed the folder and threw it back on the coffee table.

"Well, they're getting him up on his feet in the morning." Larsen pushed the positive news. "So, by the time Noah is ready to go home, Simpson should be ready to go off on a new mission."

She turned to face him. "You're joking, right? Or did you miss the whole part about PT for his shoulder? He won't be cleared for active service for months. Plus, he may be on his feet tomorrow, but I seriously doubt he's going to be doing anything more than standing upright and maybe making a circuit around his bed."

Larsen shifted so he was facing her, his hands gently holding her biceps. "What I was thinking, well—it's gonna be at least a week or maybe two before you have to do anything. Walker wants that mission debrief. He has to take it before the committee to sign off on it officially and to get support for those commendations he wants to hand out. By then, Derek should be walking pretty good."

She looked at him, a small curl of her lip, her expression showing that she believed he had slipped up. His argument was flawed. "So, he's walking, but not capable of shooting, so not ready to be cleared for active service." She caressed his cheek. "I'm sorry, Larsen. At this point, I don't trust Noah to keep his word. As soon as Derek gets to him, and he will, whatever we do, Noah'll just be back to his personal asset."

Larsen ran the tip of his tongue along his top lip. As a SEAL, he had been taught to be prepared for any situation. His walk back to Allison's office had been very long and round about. Reaching into his pants pocket, he unfolded a single page document.

"I stopped off at the communications office and while I was there, I sort of happened on this. I think it's an ideal posting for an injured spy. Just the thing to let him recover, but keep him in the game. "

He paused to take a deep breath while handing her the page. "It would involve you convincing Walker to put Derek up for a promotion."

Deep down, Allison Peterson had known she was in trouble the second her hand had involuntarily gone to James Larsen's cheek. She had let her defenses down completely when he had looked at her with his warm, honest, brown eyes, holding her attention as his tongue had flickered out to wet his top lip. She didn't even see where the neatly folded sheet of paper came from. In fact, it wasn't until he spoke in that smooth as silk tone that she realized she had walked straight into his trap.

Allison Peterson had known James Larsen for over fifteen years; she knew exactly how determined he got when taking on a cause. She had thought she had prepared herself for whatever scheme he would come up with to sweet-talk her into helping out Noah Wolf, but she had not seen this coming. He had to be crazy.

"Promotion? You want me to get that evil son of a bitch Simpson a promotion?" She snatched her hand away from where it had been caressing his cheek and sat back on the couch, her eyes quickly scanning the single page document.

"It's a mission brief for a diplomatic posting," Larsen told her helpfully. "The UN Security Council is sending a team to monitor the situation in India. There's going to be envoys from Russia and China there, too."

"I can read, Larsen," she snapped. "You really think that this," she shook the page in his face, "is a good idea?"

He caught hold of her wrist and then took the piece of paper out of her hand. "Derek speaks both Russian and Hindi fluently, he understands Russian foreign policy and he'd be able to keep an eye on what the Russkies and the Chinese are up to. Walker would love it. I bet it would be really easy for you to talk him into it. I'd even be willing to bet he takes it to the committee as his own idea."

She snatched the page back and finished reading the mission brief. "It'd be like inviting a fox into the hen house," she muttered, shaking her head in refusal. "I'm not going to be held responsible for this." She had a vision of Derek taking it upon himself to sort out the diplomatic wrangling with a few well placed bullets.

"Of course not, you're not even CIA. Derek would be part of the U.S. envoy's team. It would just be a little light bodyguard work," Larsen pointed out as if reading her mind.

"You're joking, right?" she huffed and crossed her arms over her chest, her eyes never leaving his as she thought things through.

The trouble was, as crazy as Larsen's plan was, it did have some merit. Sending Derek off to India was tempting. If he didn't get kidnapped or assassinated by rival covert agents, there was always the chance that he would be caught in a bombing raid. Most important in her mind, though, was that he would be far too busy to be keeping tabs on what Noah Wolf was up to.

But the plan also required her to contact Alex Walker and suggest that she thought Derek deserved a promotion to India as well as a commendation and a nice easy mission while he recuperated. The whole thought of calling that man and asking him for a favor made her skin crawl.

"You have quite a mean streak, Commander Larsen." She

finally broke eye contact. "You really missed your calling. Are you sure you don't want come work with me at E&E?"

"No, thanks," he laughed, drinking in her figure as she got to her feet.

"Of course, all your plotting relies on the Indian people keeping up their civil war until Derek is fit enough for the job and Walker approving the posting." She disappeared into the kitchen, and when she came out, she held two open bottles of German beer in her hands. "Did you know that idiot once made a pass at me?" She shook her head in disgust. "I guess I could do a little flirting if I had to, but..."

Handing Larsen one of the bottles, she sat down next to him. "Now, let's suppose for the sake of argument that the Indian people keep fighting and Alex Walker can be talked into sending his pet wet work specialist off on a diplomatic mission, what am I supposed to do with Noah? God only knows how long it'll be before he's fit for any kind of duty, and he may never be able to handle going back to wet work."

She waited for his comeback and, then, when he didn't answer her straight away, she assumed he was stumped. "Give it up, Larsen. The best I can do for Noah is to take him home and try to find a place to use him." She took a long sip from the bottle. "The problem will be his team. I doubt any of them will be able or willing to work with anyone else."

Larsen drained the bottle in one long gulp and then lounged back comfortably on the couch in a completely relaxed pose. "You agree to the plan in principle, though?" He smiled softly, but she was on guard now and could see the sharpness in his eyes.

"Sending Simpson off to India to be somebody else's problem? Yes. It's a good plan, even if it does require me to make nice with that asshole Walker." She shrugged. It had been a stimulating conversation, but it had led nowhere.

"You can do it," Larsen spoke up. "You can bring Noah back, Allie, I know you can."

"But how? Noah..." She stopped and ran her hands over her

face, then looked at him again. "James, you didn't know him before this. Noah was the perfect assassin; no emotions, no conscience at all, but a finely devised moral code that he would never violate. On one mission, he was supposed to eliminate an entire drug cartel family, but he couldn't justify to himself the necessity of killing two small children who would have been legitimate collateral damage. He went off-mission and kidnapped them and their nanny, forced me to arrange for the kids to be adopted and the nanny to get a new identity. There's no way he would have allowed something like this to happen."

Larsen shook his head. "I just don't get how Simpson could mess him up that much in the short time they were together. Something had to have happened, Allie, something that broke whatever made him that way."

"Something we don't know about," Allison said. "Maybe that's the key we need to find. If we knew what caused Noah to lose that emotional wall of his, there might be some hope for him yet."

"You said it yourself, he was a good agent until he was teamed up with Simpson. We just need to find a way to bring him back to that point, get him to shake off whatever Simpson did to him."

Allison nodded. "Okay, then let's find out what it is we don't know. If we can learn what happened to Noah, and if we can find some way to undo it, and if Simpson can be kept away from him, then we might have a chance to actually bring him back into the fold."

"That's a lot of ifs, Allie." Larsen looked doubtful.

She set her empty bottle down next to Larsen's, a determined look on her face. "Well, it's the best I can come up with. The problem is, I'm going to need more help than just you."

She reached out and picked up her cell phone, dialing a number quickly from memory.

"Nathan? It's Allison. I need you to do something for me." She quickly outlined what she wanted and waited for an acknowledgment, then hung up without a goodbye. She looked at the phone for a moment before putting it down again, then turned her attention back to Larsen. "That's done. Now, I suggest we stop talking about Simpson and Noah and get some rest." She came toward him in slow, measured steps. "What do you say?"

Larsen knew when to back off. Allison had some kind of plan in mind for saving Noah Wolf's ass. "I'm not sure about rest being the right word, Allie." He pulled her into a tight embrace, their lips locking in a passionate kiss.

FIFTEEN

D OCTOR N ATHAN P ARKER SCOWLED AT THE PHONE AS he hung up, then looked at the door leading out of his office. "Kathy!" he shouted. "Get in here!"

His secretary came rushing in a second later. "Yes, Doctor Parker?"

"I want you to call Donnie Jefferson and tell him to get Team Camelot to the airfield within an hour. Tell him I also want the biggest damned airplane he's got, because we need to get over to Sigonella as soon as humanly possible. Sooner, if he can figure out a way to make that happen." He reached for his phone again, then stopped and looked up at his secretary as she was about to hurry out the door. "And then call Wally Lawson and tell him I'm coming to see him."

Kathy stopped and glanced back. "Yes, sir," she said, and then she was gone.

Parker got up from his desk and hurried out the door, not bothering to stop as he hurried past his secretary's desk. He could feel her eyes watching him as he exited the building, but her curiosity wasn't important to him at the moment. What he wanted to do was get out to R&D and talk the problem over with Wally before he had to get on a plane and fly to Italy.

His car was waiting in the parking lot where it always was, the big, old 1972 Buick Riviera that he had bought new the day he graduated with his doctorate. He climbed in and started up the huge engine, put the car in reverse and backed out of his parking place, then pushed his foot to the floor as he headed toward R&D.

Wally was waiting for him at the front door of the building. When Parker climbed out of the big car, Wally came rushing over.

"Doc!" Wally said. "What in the world brings you out here?"

"I need to pick your brain," Parker said. "Allison just called me. She says Noah has lost whatever it was he had that made him a walking computer. I'm trying to think of a way to help him get it back. Any ideas?"

Wally's eyes were wide and round. "Noah? You got to be kidding me. Oh my gosh, Doc, this is a disaster."

"You're telling me this? Noah Wolf is the best assassin we've ever found, and that's because emotions can't dominate his thoughts or actions. He plans a mission based on a logical understanding of the situation and carries it out without any kind of emotion involved. It makes him more able to focus on what he's doing than anyone else, and it's probably the reason he and his team have survived the missions they have."

Wally made a *tsk* sound. "Most of them, anyway. None of us will ever forget Moose Conway. He didn't survive his last mission."

Parker nodded. "Yes, but that illustrates my point. Moose died because he made an emotion-based decision, he drew a killer's fire away from the other kid, the computer nerd. Noah saw it all happen, knew exactly what Moose was doing, and still kept his own attention focused on taking the killer out. He didn't let an emotional reaction take him away from his mission."

Wally scowled. "Okay, okay, I get it. Still, if Noah's lost it..."

"Look, Wally," Parker said, "I know you guys get into some psych research out here, so I'm sure you've got all the files on what happened to Noah when he was a kid. No doubt in my mind

Allison has asked you to look for ways to create the same condition in others, so tell me what you've learned."

Wally hesitated for only a second, then turned and motioned for the psychiatrist to follow him. They walked right past the security desk and into the bowels of the building, turning down a hall that led off to the right as soon as they got past the lobby area.

"This is the biggest secret lab out here," Wally said. "None of the teams ever come here, because we don't want anyone to have any foreknowledge of anything we develop here. Our most recent avenues into reduction of emotional bias—that's what we call it, anyway—is through a modified vipassana approach. Are you familiar with vipassana?"

Parker nodded. "Self evaluation through deep meditation. Right? I've read some articles..."

"That's what the medical community thinks it is," Wally said, "but it's far more than that. Vipassana involves genuinely looking at who and what you are, actually seeing the real self instead of the one we imagine ourselves to be. It means facing every fear, every unsated desire, every area where we just don't know a part of ourselves, and then releasing any claim on them. It's been shown to be effective in treating depression, anxiety, panic, just about every emotional disorder there is, and it does so by removing the importance of our emotions from our lives."

Parker shook his head. "Sounds like a long term procedure," he said. "Noah may not have that much time. Wally, considering that Noah is one of the death row recruits, if his abilities are gone, Allison will have to order his elimination. As long as he's serving the country as an assassin, the risk that someone will find out he's still alive is worth taking, but if he's no longer able, then he's just a liability she can't afford."

Wally sucked in his cheeks. "Then we have to move fast," he said. "The thing I was leading up to is that we've found a way to make vipassana work a lot faster, but it isn't pleasant, and if we were talking about anything other than saving Noah, I wouldn't even sanction using it on a human being, but it's the only thing I can imagine being able to do what you want." He stopped and turned to the old doctor. "Just one thing," he said. "Swear to me you'll never tell anyone I gave it to you."

Parker's eyes narrowed, but he nodded. "You have my word. Now, what is it?"

Wally sighed. "We call it methetrax," he said. "And I hope we never have to let the FDA get a look at it."

———

SARAH AND JENNY were sitting on the sofa while Neil was at the kitchen table, computer open as he searched for any way to hack into the medical database at Sigonella's Naval Hospital. The problem wasn't that it had particularly good security, but that whoever ran the database didn't seem to know what they were doing. Information contained in it had no defined sturcture, so he wasn't finding any references to Noah at all.

All three of them jumped when their phones went off simultaneously, and all three looked at the text message that had come in. Neil was the first to speak as he hurried into the living room.

"Did you girls get..." He trailed off as he saw both of them getting to their feet.

Team Camelot, the message read, *all members pack and report to Kirtland airfield. Dispatch to assist Director with Camelot recovery efforts.*

"What the hell does that mean?" Sarah asked. "Camelot recovery efforts?"

"It means," Jenny said, "Allie needs us to help bring Noah back. Come on, let me help you pack some stuff..."

Sarah shook her head. "I've got a go-bag, Noah says we should always have one packed and ready. It's in the closet over there."

Jenny hugged her. "Good," she said. "Neil and I can get packed in ten minutes, and then we'll head to the airport. Chin up, Sarah, you'll be seeing Noah in a few hours."

Sarah looked up at her. "Yeah," she said. "But will it really be him?"

"Of course it will," Neil said. "He's Noah. No matter what he's going through, he's still Noah."

DEREK SIMPSON WAS STILL SMILING about his sudden insight into the private life of Allison Peterson after his encounter with the couple in the hallway. Even being moved to another, more secure room hadn't dampened his spirits. He knew the Dragon Lady's game. She would keep up the pretense of control right up to the moment she had to stand in front of him and Noah and hand them their medals.

He was looking forward to that moment; the image of that damned controlling bitch finally being put in her place improved his mood even more. It was just a shame he couldn't get word to Noah. Sharing that bit of intel about the SEAL and the Dragon Lady would be sure to brighten up the kid's day.

He was brought out of his musings when the door to his room opened and one of the guards stepped inside, accompanying a much older nurse than the easily manipulated Angie Morrison.

"Well, hello, darlin', and how are you this morning?" He beamed at his new nurse.

"I'm fine, Agent Simpson, but if you call me 'darlin'' one more time, I just might have to report you for sexual harrassment. Hashtag me too, you know?" She returned his suddenly faltering smile with one of her own. "Now, let's get you into this wheelchair and down to the PT unit."

Derek turned his eyes from the nurse to the guard, who stared stonily back at him. The young man had been on the receiving end of Derek's sarcasm since the beginning of his shift.

"Anything you say, my dear," Derek answered smoothly. Once he was up on his feet, he would show everybody who was in charge.

THE FIRST NOAH knew about a change in his circumstances was when James Larsen strolled into his room and switched on the overhead light, causing the normally dim room to be suddenly bright.

Letting out a groan, Noah threw an arm protectively over his eyes and tried to disappear under the sheet covering his body. He wanted to be left alone in his misery. He didn't want any more sympathy and understanding. He wasn't used to it and it just left him more confused than ever.

He was having trouble figuring out why he had broken down the way he did, and something told him Derek would have sneered at his weakness. He hated to think about what others would think of him, especially the people closest to him. It just hadn't been like him at all, and he couldn't understand why it had happened.

"Hey, Noah. Time to get up."

The sheet was jerked off his head and he found himself squinting up into Larsen's no-nonsense expression.

"Hey!" he complained. "What'd I do now?"

"Nothing. It's just time for you to stop laying around here, moping and feeling sorry for yourself." Larsen dropped a heavy pile of manuals down on the trolley tray that still held the remains of Noah's half eaten breakfast. "What you need is something to take your mind off things."

With his hands free, Larsen helped Noah to sit up. "C'mon, let's get you up. I've got some reading material for you."

"You don't have to do this," Noah spoke in a soft voice, but he was too tired to argue, so he reached over and picked up the top book on the pile.

"What's this?" he asked with a frown.

Larsen peered over and read the title. "That one is the latest copy of the International Code of Conduct," he answered calmly.

Noah spread the manuals out over the tray top, his eyes going from one to another.

They were all training manuals he remembered from the classrooms he'd been sent to after Allison had recruited him. He stared up at the stony-faced SEAL.

"Again, what is this? I mean, what am I supposed to do with it? I finished all my training three years ago." He pushed everything away and lay back, folding his arms over his chest.

"You need to be up on all this stuff if you get the assignment your boss is considering for you," Larsen answered calmly.

Noah's eyes went wide. "Assignment? You did it? You got the Dra... I mean, Allison is gonna let me stay?" Noah asked eagerly. For the first time since he'd had his meeting with Allison, he felt a small sliver of hope. He hadn't really believed Larsen would be able to help him.

"It depends on a few things. I mean, your boss, Ms. Peterson, is not in a particularly forgiving mood, Noah. You're gonna have to work hard to impress her." Larsen had caught the Dragon Lady comment and had been forced to stifle a grin. Everyone called her the Dragon Lady, it seemed.

"What does she want me to do?" Noah's eyes strayed to the books again. "Take a test?"

"She has rules. First off, she's real insistent that you have no more contact with Derek Simpson; you don't speak to him, if you see him coming toward you in the hallway, you go in the other direction. If he gets a call through, you hang up. He's been a pretty bad influence on you, buddy."

Noah nodded slowly. He could do that. Or at least he thought he could. There was still a small part of him that didn't trust that anybody could help him other than Derek.

"Second, you go back home to Neverland. She's gonna use your head wound as a reason to take you off active service for a while. It'll get you clear of Derek and give you a chance to recuperate properly."

"For how long?" Something in the back of his head started to get excited, but he pushed it down before he could even recognize what it was. Back to Neverland? Larsen had spoken of an assignment, now he was talking about some kind of extended leave back at HQ.

"For as long as she thinks it takes for you to get your head straight," Larsen said.

"She's gonna take me back home and just leave me on the inactive list," Noah said. "How is that going to do me any good? If they decide I'm not worth keeping, I'll end up in the potter's field." He had a brief mental image of Jackson, the former PT instructor who had been caught betraying E&E. The potter's field was what they called the unmarked graves where traitors and other unwanted bodies were disposed of.

"I am helping you. That is what all this is for." Larsen gestured to the book pile. "She wants to put you in as a training instructor for a while, until you can get your head back on straight and be worth sending out on missions again."

Noah felt a surge of some other unknown emotion, panic at the thought of being responsible for training the new recruits. He was a field assassin; just his name caused fear in intelligence circles. Having to train new recruits was for those who couldn't handle it out in the field.

"No, I can't! What the hell is she thinking? If I don't make it as an instructor, it just makes it easier for her to get rid of me and she can say she tried. No, absolutely not. How the hell can I train anybody?"

I told ya, kid. That bitch Peterson is out to get you. She's playing games. She can't stand the fact you did such a good job. Just leave it to me. I'll straighten it all out.

SIXTEEN

"Hey, Noah!" Larsen said. "Noah! Snap out of it."

Noah jumped as Larsen's voice broke through his panic. Taking a deep, shuddering breath, he collapsed back against the pillows. "If she's gonna sideline me, I might as well be terminated." He shoved the bed tray away from him.

"That's not it at all, Noah," Larsen said. "What she wants is for you to remember how to do your job, the way you used to. You were the best she had, Noah, but it was because of who you were. We don't know what's happened, but you're not the same guy you used to be. What she's hoping this will accomplish is that you'll figure out what happened and get back to being yourself again."

Don't trust that wet rag Larsen. What's he ever done for you, kid? Noah did his best to block out the sound of Derek whispering in his ear, advising him to tell the SEAL to go screw himself. He had no reason to doubt Larsen's word. He forced himself to listen to the man who was actually in the room with him, rather than the ghost of the one who wasn't.

"It'll be okay. Allison really wants what's best for you, Noah. So do a lot of other people."

Noah suddenly stared at him. "Other people?" he asked. "What other people?"

"Noah, have you completely forgotten your team? What about your wife, have you forgotten about her?"

Noah lowered his eyes to his hands. "No, of course not," he said. "I haven't forgotten anybody. I just don't know what good I'm going to be to them anymore, you know?"

Larsen cocked his head to the side. It almost sounded like Noah was about ready to start talking. If he could find out what really happened in Germany, even before the massacre at Reitner's place, maybe there was something they could do to help Noah after all.

"And why is that, Noah?" he asked. "Why can't you go back to being Allison's number one guy? What happened to you that took away that cold, emotionless demeanor you always had?"

The buzzing in his head started up, and Noah had to close his eyes to try to force it back. Every time he tried to think about what had happened, the buzzing began. This time, it was even worse than before.

Larsen caught it and leaned closer. "Noah? What's the matter, what's going on?"

Noah's head snapped up, his eyes narrowed and his expression became icy. He stared at Larsen through a fine red mist of anger. As his lip curled into a snarl, the thought crossed his mind that if he had been armed, James Larsen would have been in serious trouble. Noah would have dearly loved to slip a knife into him, but he had no idea why.

As fast as the anger flared, it dissipated, replaced with disgust. He was having murderous thoughts about the only person who was willing to help him. He deserved whatever was going to happen to him. Turning away from the SEAL, Noah stared fixedly at the far wall, hoping Larsen would get the message and just go.

There was the rattle of the trolley being moved back in front of him and then the sound of a hand slamming down on the books. The noise made Noah flinch and drew his attention back to the older man.

"Noah, I want you to look at me when I'm talkin' to you." Larsen had had enough of quiet understanding. Noah Wolf was wallowing in some kind of self-pity and needed to be jerked out of it. "Have you forgotten I was with you for the whole forty-eight hours after we dragged you outta that hole? I know what you and Simpson did, so if I was you, I'd be grateful for this chance to prove I'm more than just a murderous bastard. Now, we know something happened to you that messed with your head. What we need to know is what it was, so that we can try to figure out what to do about it."

Noah stared at the SEAL. He had never seen Larsen so pissed off before, but he couldn't bring himself to speak. Nothing was going the way he thought it would. He was in completely unfamiliar territory. Wolves were never known to apologize, even if they were in the wrong, and Noah wasn't going to take being called names by anybody.

He shot a glance at Larsen's stern expression and the cold eyes that were staring down at him. He was suddenly reminded of a large drill sergeant he'd known during basic training. Slowly, without saying a word, Noah reached out and pulled the first book off the pile before him.

———

ALLISON PACED in front of her desk, her arms folded over her chest and her head bowed in concentration. She had been putting off making the call all day, but finally, she could put it off no longer. She looked at the phone sitting on her desk, her eyes narrowing before she turned away and continued trying to wear a hole in the floor.

It was ridiculous, it really was. She wasn't afraid of anybody. How could making this one phone call have her so shaken up? Admittedly, the man was a creep and made her skin crawl, but he was on the other end of a phone, a few thousand miles away, at least.

She rubbed at her arms and came to a stop. She was getting angry with herself, as well as with James Larsen for forcing her to agree to make the call. She looked at her watch. It was three p.m., which meant it was ten a.m. in D.C. She was running out of excuses.

Damn Noah Wolf, and damn James Larsen for convincing her she might be able to save Noah after all.

Moving around the desk to her chair, she sat down and pulled the phone in front of her. She was an intelligent, grown woman. Never mind that she had once been the nerdy girl in school, the one nobody ever took seriously. Those days were long past, and she had grown out of it during high school. By the time she got to college, she already knew that a career with the CIA was what she wanted.

Of course, she hadn't reckoned with the possibility of being handed her own agency to run. That only happened in story-books, right? The lowly CIA intelligence analyst displays a tenacious ability to know when the elimination of a particular individual could alter the course of international relations, reliably for the better. Hell, if we give her a black ops budget and enough people to take out anybody who gets in the way, we have a chance to make the world a better place, right?

That was the logic used by the former president in creating her post, and it was usually considered by those who knew about her that she had been doing her job quite well. The rest of the world, if they knew about her at all, should be afraid of her.

So, what was she scared of? She wasn't scared; scared was the wrong word. She was just not sure that the call she was about to make was the right one.

Picking up the phone, she took a calming breath. "Michael, get me Alex Walker, please. His number is on the list."

Leaning back, she watched the phone; taking deep, slow breaths, she waited for it to ring. Unfortunately, she didn't have long to wait. Picking up the handset, she forced a smile onto her face, knowing that he would be able to hear it.

"Alex, sir. Thank you for taking my call." She spoke warmly, hoping she could keep the call as short as possible.

"Ah, Ms. Peterson, to what do I owe the pleasure of hearing your sweet voice?" The syrupy voice of the CIA Director made her skin crawl.

"I just wanted to be sure you received Agent Simpson's debrief, Alex." She hid her dislike as best she could.

"Why, yes, I actually did, my dear, and the recommendation for the awards, as well. As I told the oversight committee, I was sure it would be coming soon, and I was glad that you didn't let me down. I truly appreciate you getting it done so quickly."

Allison had to relax her jaw before she could speak. "Thank you for your understanding, Alex..." How did that man ever get appointed to his position?

"Not a problem, not a problem at all. Now, if there is nothing else, I really am rather busy..."

She spoke quickly, before he could hang up. "Actually, Alex, I was hoping to talk to you about Agent Simpson."

"Oh, yes, I heard something about Derek causing some sort of problem with one of the nurses." The sound of his deep chuckle came through the handset.

"Oh, that was only something minor, and easily handled. I wanted to talk to you about a posting that recently came empty, one that I think would be ideal for him."

There was silence on the line for a moment. She thought she could hear muffled voices in the background and then he was back.

"Pardon me, my dear, a job for Derek? I believe I just read in your report that he is recovering from a couple of gunshot wounds. Isn't that right?"

She could tell he had his guard up. Alex Walker liked to come across as a simple good old boy, but she knew that hiding behind that easy going exterior was a razor sharp mind and cold, hard ambition.

"Yes, you're right, of course, but he is going to be up on his feet in the next week and I think such a valuable asset to the Company should be utilized at every opportunity. The job only requires him to sit and watch, but he would be watching high level Chinese and Russian diplomats. I'm sure you want somebody in that position who could handle it, and I think Derek is perfect for the job."

"Are you referring to the problems in India? Please correct me if I'm wrong here, but I wasn't aware that your agency had any sort of connection to that region."

"Of course we do, we have people almost everywhere. Granted, this is a CIA matter rather than one for my organization, but I was sure you would be looking at the big picture. With all those diplomats meeting in one place, it seemed to me that it might be wise to have somebody from our intelligence services over there to monitor how the friendship between the Russians and Chinese was developing, and I would just like to put Agent Simpson's name forward. He has quite a great deal of experience in the region." She closed her eyes and swallowed thickly, trying to hold down her lunch.

"Why, Ms. Peterson, I'm surprised to find that you care about Agent Simpson. Has his boyish charm managed to capture your attention?"

Her eyes flew open wide. "Why would you think that...?" Oh, James Larsen was going to pay dearly for talking her into this, and so was Noah, if he put one foot out of line after she did this for him.

"That particular job would take him out of the field, at least for the most part, and he'd need a higher security clearance. I have to give him a promotion to get his rank high enough. Of course, being out of the field would mean he was safer, certainly a consideration if there might be any sort of romantic relationship with his future."

"I don't think that is relevant." She didn't want to give him the opportunity to take the conversation down that route. "You suggested that I should consider their fine efforts and reward good work, remember? I'm just taking your advice to heart. Don't you think this would be a perfect opportunity for him?"

"I'll confess that the idea has some merit." He was clearly enjoying himself. "Let me take some time to think over your proposal and I'll get back to you. The medals should be approved sometime during the next week. I'm thinking a nice, quiet ceremony with some pictures to show our new German friends. Doesn't that seem appropriate to you?"

"Thank you, Alex. I'll make sure you get the pictures as soon as Derek and Noah receive those medals." Her stomach almost turned as she realized she was feeding his disgusting assumption that she found Derek Simpson somehow appealing. The people in her position often had to do things they didn't want to do. If it got Simpson away from Noah, it would almost be worth the rumors that would be flying around Capitol Hill about her in the future.

With a sigh, she dropped the phone down onto the cradle and looked up to find Larsen watching her from the doorway.

"That man makes me ill," she growled. "You owe me big for making that call."

Larsen grinned. "Did he go for it?"

"I think so," she said with a sigh. "I'm sure at the next committee meeting, he'll suddenly come up with the brilliant idea of putting one of his people into the U.S. envoy's team. All we can hope for is that he goes ahead and gives the job to Derek." She looked up at him. "How did it go with Noah?"

"Still feeling sorry for himself, but he's willing to take the posting as an instructor. He doesn't want to, but that could be a good thing."

"That's good. Keeping him busy might be part of the answer."

"I'll make sure he knows it, Allie. I don't think that will be any problem, but there's something else."

"And what would that be?"

"I took a shot. I mentioned to Noah that he used to be the best, but that something seemed to have happened that took away his emotional detachment. When I said that, I was hoping he might open up about other things that took place during the mission, but what I saw was a man who seemed to be suffering from a sudden migraine. Eyes clamped shut, he put a hand to his head, and I'll swear he looked like he was dizzy for just a moment."

"Dizzy?" Allison's eyes narrowed. "Larsen, did you get any sort of idea what might have caused that?"

"I'm afraid not," he said. "When he came out of it, he was so angry I half expected him to come off the bed and attack me, but then he calmed right down. If anything, I think he looked ashamed. I don't know what happened to him, but I would just about bet that it involved some sort of chemicals."

Allison stared at him for a moment. "Chemicals," she repeated. "He's been drugged? What the hell kind of drug can make such a drastic change in an already affected personality?"

"Hey, I'm not the guy to ask. When do your reinforcements arrive? Maybe some of them will have ideas."

"Not for a couple of hours, yet. They landed at Heathrow about an hour ago, but it's going to take a little time to get the shuttle flight set up. Somehow, the orders for a diplomatic flight from London got lost in the shuffle." She got to her feet and leaned on the desk for a moment. "I need a shower. I swear Walker oozes slime through the phone line; just talking to him makes me feel dirty."

Larsen grinned at her. "Well, if you need any help washing your back..."

"Shut up, Larsen," she said playfully as she stepped into the outer office.

SEVENTEEN

She stopped in front of Agent Logan's desk. "Logan, are you up for a secret mission?"

"Yes, ma'am!" He snapped to attention, his chair falling over backwards in his rush to get to his feet.

"It's okay, Logan, take it easy. Sometime in the next hour, a call is going to be patched through to you, because I won't be available. A man with a deep voice is going to demand you allow him to speak to Agent Simpson. I want you to let the call through, but not immediately. I want you to make him think you are doing it against my orders. Understand?"

"Ma'am, this man, is it Alex Walker? Isn't he the CIA Director?"

"Agent Logan, part of a field operative's job is to lie convincingly. If you feel uncomfortable doing this work..." She let the sentence hang in the air.

"No, ma'am, I don't have any problem with it at all."

Allison smiled at him. "Good, now I'm going to my quarters. Just remember, let him bully you into allowing the call, but not too quickly. I want him to think he really pulled a fast one."

———

HALF AN HOUR LATER, while Allison was in the shower scrubbing away the oily feeling she got from talking to Alex Walker, with the assistance of James Larsen, Agent Logan was fielding a call put through to him from the surgical ward nurses' station.

After ten minutes of hesitation and awkwardness, he finally agreed that Alex had the authority to overrule Allison and ordered the nursing staff to put his call through to Agent Simpson. Afterward, he leaned back in his chair, a wide smile almost splitting his face in two. He had just completed his first field assignment for Director Peterson. Hopefully it was just the first of many.

———

ALLISON SIGHED and closed her eyes, resting back against James Larsen's bare chest as warm water cascaded down over their bodies. She nestled her head into the crook of his neck, a sultry smile curving her lips as he whispered sweet words into her ear.

The combination of the warm water relaxing her muscles and Larsen's strong hands softly kneading her flesh worked to clear away all thoughts of rogue spies and slimy bureaucrats from her mind. Thoroughly relaxed and with a feeling of tranquility settling over her, she surrendered to Larsen's touch completely as he cocooned her in his arms, his lips pressing teasingly soft kisses along her jaw.

"I think we should take this to the bed—" His words, made husky by desire, were suddenly cut off by a loud, annoying and incessant sound.

Her phone rang at that moment, and Allison looked around to where it lay on the counter.

"Allie, baby, leave it." He tried to block her hand from reaching up to turn off the water.

"Larsen, I have—" With the tap turned off, Allison slid open the condensation-covered glass shower door.

The phone continued ringing.

"Hey, c'mon now, Allie—dammit." He reached for her one last time, but she twisted out of his grip and picked up her phone.

With a huff, Larsen followed her out of the shower and, after wrapping a towel around his waist, he picked up another and enclosed her in a thick, fluffy bath towel.

"Logan," she said. "Has Alex called?" She leaned back against Larsen's chest as he gently rubbed his hands over the towel, helping her to dry off.

"Yes, ma'am," Logan said. "I did as you said and put the call through after letting him talk me into going against your orders, but afterward, he called back and demanded that I remove the guard from Agents Simpson and Wolf's doors. I tried to tell him..." The young agent's voice came through the phone loud enough that Larsen could hear every word.

"It's okay, I was expecting it," Allison replied, halting the young man's speech. "Just do as he ordered and remove the guards from outside both rooms."

"Ma'am?"

She felt Larsen stiffen and back away from her, but she was in full business mode and couldn't concern herself with hurting his feelings.

"It's not a complicated order, Logan. Remove the guards from outside Simpson's and Noah's doors, and then when Simpson goes to PT, you go in and plant at least one listening device either on or near his bed. Then you do the same again when Noah is out of his room. And do not speak to anybody else about what you are doing. Is that clear?"

"Yes, ma'am."

"Good, now get to it." Ending the call, Allison turned just in time to catch sight of Larsen's back as he left the bathroom.

Deep down, she had known that allowing their relationship to start up again was a bad idea. It had been a couple of years since they had last hooked up, but Larsen was the only person outside her organization whom she completely trusted. They had history together, they knew each other's darkest secrets, and Larsen actually managed to make her feel loved, something she'd rarely experienced.

When they reached her quarters, she had felt Larsen's breath on her neck as she unlocked the door. Stepping inside, she turned, barring him from following.

"We can't let this continue, Larsen. Simpson knows, or at least suspects. I can't become the talk of the intelligence community, and that's where this would lead." She continued to block his entry into her quarters and he had just stared back at her with pain in his eyes.

"Look, let me come in, at least while we talk. Keeping me out here in the hall is going to draw even more attention than anything we do in private."

He was right, but letting him inside was only going to lead to him staying the night. The trouble was, she couldn't bring herself to slam the door in his face either. It had been over a year since she had spoken to a man about anything other than work.

Then, as if he was reading her mind, he had leaned in a little closer. "Why don't we go stay off base? Catania is only a few miles away. It's a big city, lots of people, lots of hotels."

She pressed the edge of her cell phone against her forehead; she had honestly thought Larsen would understand the situation. Muttering an expletive, she turned and walked inside, leaving him to follow. He stepped in and stood on the far side of the room, his back to her, but she didn't need to see his face to know how angry he was. The emotion was coming off him in waves.

"Okay, I just don't get it," he said. "Taking the guards off means Simpson can get to Noah again. What good is it going to do to bug the rooms? If Derek talks to Noah, the damage will already be done."

"Jesus, Larsen, I shouldn't have to explain this to you. Removing the guards is going to make Derek believe he's won and it also means I can make sure Noah isn't just stringing us along before I have to hand him a commendation."

He glanced back at her, his normally warm brown eyes cold

and hard. "You're as good as setting Noah up to fail. That kid is at a crossroads. You shouldn't be allowing Derek anywhere near him."

"You're the one who told me Noah had his head on straight, that he'd stick to the deal. I'm just getting confirmation." With all her clothes in place, Allison picked up her hairbrush, running it through her damp hair and dragging it mercilessly through any tangles.

"Like I said before, you're setting him up." He sat on the edge of the bed lacing up his boots, his movements jerky as he fought to control his temper.

"Larsen." She sighed out his name, turning to look at him directly. "You can't protect Noah indefinitely. Sooner or later, Simpson is going to get to him and when he does, I need to be sure I can trust him to do the right thing. If he can't turn Derek down now, when everything that happened is still fresh in his mind, what's the chance Simpson won't get to him later? Then what happens? How long before they do something that can't be covered up?"

Larsen was back on his feet now, the scowl slowly slipping away as he stared back into her blue eyes. He hated that she had a point, but Noah Wolf was an accomplished agent, which made him a skilled liar. The only way to be sure that he was telling the truth was to set him up and see what he did.

Larsen scowled. "This is what I hate about spooks. Nothing is ever simple and straight with any of you."

"It's not just about being simple. It's because we live in a world full of deception that we have to go to such extremes to get to the truth. Noah has been trained to pick up from a single look what it will take to get you on his side. He is capable of looking you right in the eye and telling you black is white and you'll believe him." Allison took a step closer and then another one until she was in front of him. They stood within arm's reach of each other, but not touching.

"I have to be certain, Larsen. It's not just my career that's on the line. What happens if we don't stop Simpson now? How many more innocent people are going to become collateral damage because they got in his way? If Noah is wanting to be his loyal little protégé, I need to know it now."

She searched his face, looking for some sign of his affection for her and was rewarded as the tension slowly left his body and a hint of a smile broke the harsh, straight line of his mouth. It was her turn to surrender a little of her anger as his hand came up to gently move a couple of damp strands of hair away from her face.

"I still think you're going about this the wrong way."

"And I think this is the only way to be sure," she replied, a smile causing the corners of her eyes to crinkle. "Can we just agree to disagree on this and go do something to keep our minds off the subject of Simpson and Noah?"

"What did you have in mind?" he asked, his eyes dropping to focus on her fingers as they slowly began to unbutton his shirt.

———

"I don't know why he's here," Sarah whispered, casting her eyes at Parker as they waited for the shuttle flight to board. "He's never come out in the field before."

"No, but he's our top shrink," Marco replied just as softly. "If Noah's having a problem, maybe he's exactly what we need." Renée leaned toward Sarah. "He's probably just along to see that we don't say or do anything to upset Noah. If he's lost his ability to hold back his emotions, he could be pretty unstable. I'd imagine they want to be sure we don't cause more problems."

Sarah glared at her. "I don't care what kind of problems Noah has," she hissed, "he's still my husband, and no one is going to tell me what I can and can't say to him. Not Parker, not Allison, nobody!" Renée frowned. "That's not what I…"

"You kids know I have hearing aids, right?" Parker said loudly. "You didn't think I would turn down the volume at a time like this, did you? I can hear you all just fine."

Neil snickered while the rest of them suddenly looked embarrassed, but Parker went on.

"I'm here because we have to help Noah find himself again," he said. "I've been looking into ways to do that, but mostly I want to see what happens when he comes face to face with you guys again. That may be enough to snap him out of whatever this is, but if it isn't, then I'm prepared to try some other things. Noah is far too valuable an asset to lose, but..."

"He's a lot more than an asset," Sarah said angrily, but Jenny put a hand on her shoulder and pulled her back.

Parker let out a sigh. "As I was saying," he continued, "he's too valuable an asset, but he's also a part of our family. Allison cares about your team as if you were her own kids, and even I feel closer to all of you than to any other agents we have. If there's any way to salvage Noah, I want to be smack in the middle of it. I would've come even without Allison's orders."

"I'm sorry," Sarah said. "I guess I'm just—I'm just being overprotective of him."

"Nothing wrong with that, my dear. Just be sure you don't put undue pressure on him. If he's honestly lost the emotional blockage he was suffering, then he's probably had a nervous breakdown. The last thing we need to do is make it worse, right? Be sure you don't ask him to do anything he's not capable of, don't do anything to make him feel like he's failing you, somehow. I'm afraid that might set him even further back, especially from you, Sarah. Regardless of what anyone thinks, Noah has a deep emotional investment in you. And anybody else, we would say he was in love, but the very disorder that keeps him from showing emotion the way most of us do is what makes his emotional investment even deeper than the romantic feelings one of us might experience."

Jenny squeezed Sarah's arm and leaned close. "See? I always told you Noah loves you more than anyone else's ever been loved, and now you just got it from the expert."

Sarah wiped away the tears that were brimming over from her eyes. A moment later, the loudspeaker called all of their names.

———

"Leave it to me, Derek," Walker had said. "I'll be sure your name is the only one that goes in for the job."

"And the promotion, Alex. Don't forget the promotion." Derek beamed.

"That's right on the top of my to-do list, Derek. Now, before I forget, is there anything else I can do to make your stay there more comfortable?"

"It would be nice if you could explain to Ms. Peterson that she doesn't need to have guards watching over me or Wolf."

"No problem at all. Between you and me, I'm not always sure what she's thinking, but she seemed to have taken a shine to you."

Derek laughed. "Somehow I doubt that," he said. "More likely, she just wants me out of her hair. Getting a job like this accomplishes what she wants, but she doesn't realize how neatly it plays into my own plans."

"Well, just do your best to keep the peace with her. I don't really have control over her, you know; she has her own agency, so we are theoretically equals. I have to pull in a lot of favors if I need to force her hand on anything, and I really don't want to waste any that I don't have to."

"No problem," Derek said. "I'll play nice, at least for now."

Derek lay back in his hospital bed. This most recent conversation with Alex had been very illuminating, once he had gotten past the BS the man liked to hide behind. He had won; that bitch Peterson had finally given up the fight. He looked down at where his slippers sat on the floor. He still had six little pills which, if given all at once, would induce a nice little heart attack.

Maybe he would give the over worked little woman a present after she had handed them their awards. If the heart attack didn't kill her, it would put an end to her tenure at the head of E & E. It would put her back in D.C. behind a desk, where she belonged. Yes, he was just full of good ideas at the moment.

Half an hour later, Derek's good mood increased even further as the guard on his door took a call and then left without a word. Glancing at the clock on the wall, he checked the time. It was late and he was tired. There was plenty of time to check on Noah tomorrow and break the good news to him.

EIGHTEEN

With nothing else to take up his time, Noah was spending every waking moment going over the training manuals James Larsen had left for him. Without them, he was pretty sure he would be slowly going crazy, thinking about what he had done and what the consequences were going to be. The deaths in that German farmhouse were weighing heavily on his mind and, whenever he fell asleep, the images of Derek's victims haunted his dreams.

He still had trouble believing he was going to be reduced to training Allison's newest recruits. He stared blankly at the first page of a chapter titled Stealth Kills: Striking Without Being Seen.

An instructor. If there was one job he would never have expected to be assigned, and it wasn't one he was looking forward to at all. Training had been one of the things that he and Derek had butted heads about during the mission, and his thoughts went back to those memories.

Their safe house in Nuremberg had been in the oldest part of the city, one of many small apartments above the rows of small shops which lined the narrow, winding streets. They had already had one awkward discussion where Derek had to admit he didn't speak or understand a word of German.

Noah had shaken his head. "I speak it pretty well," he said. "You just be quiet and let me do the talking."

And that's what they had done at first. Derek had insisted on taking a drive around the city, followed by a walk along the narrow, winding streets around the neighborhood until they reached the safe house that had been prepared for them.

As soon as they arrived at the dark, musty smelling apartment, Noah had begun preparing for the mission. He could still remember the somewhat amused expression on Derek Simpson's face as he put up a map of the area on one of the walls and carefully marked the place where their target was living.

"Whatcha doin', kid?" the older man had asked when he had dug into his canvas backpack, searching for binoculars and their radio communicators.

"Surveillance, Derek. Do want the first shift or should I...?"

"You're kiddin', right?" Derek had let out a snort and picked up a flak vest, throwing it at his head. "What the hell has the Dragon Lady been doing with you people?"

"We've only driven past the place once on the way here. We need to keep an eye on it, in case Reitner decides to ditch us."

"Jeez, am I goin' to have to teach you everything? Just follow my lead, kid. We're workin' against the clock here, and we don't have time to spend a week learning the guards' schedule." Derek handed him two flash-bang grenades to go along with the vest.

He stabbed a finger over the position of the house. "I've already arranged a little distraction to draw their attention away from their boss, so while the guards are dealing with that, we're going over the fence at the back of the property."

Noah looked up at him. "What kind of distraction?" he asked.

"You don't need to worry about it," Derek said. "Like I said, it's already set up." He pointed to a spot where they had seen a blind spot on the security cameras. "Once we get inside, you're going to keep an eye out while I talk to the asset. Reitner has a lot of intel we want, and it's my job to convince him to share it up. When I'm done, we'll slip out and head back here, then wait for the next appointment to get the information he'll be bringing us."

Noah had nodded. Derek was the man in charge, so he would follow orders, whether he agreed with them or not, but then a thought struck him. "What if he's not alone? Without recon, we don't know what we could be walking into. Reitner could have a squad of soldiers waiting inside."

"Good grief," Derek had said. "Is that what they teach you at E&E, how to worry about everything? Donnie Jefferson must still be managing the training back there, he always was an idiot. You let me worry about how to make this work, kid. All you have to do is follow my orders. Just lighten up, will you? This will be fun, and maybe you'll actually learn something about what we do for a living."

Noah had learned a lot during his time in training at Neverland, but Derek was constantly running the organization down, insisting that the only way to train any kind of agent was in the field and on the job. Now, Noah was now going to be working as an instructor himself; should he turn his back on the methods that had helped him, methods he actually believed in? While Derek might have a lot more experience in the field, Noah couldn't imagine trying to teach the recruits by his methods.

He set the book down on the table unread and picked up another. This one outlined approved interrogation techniques, but after opening the first page, he put it back down. He had never liked Derek's way of getting answers, even when it worked.

Suddenly he was back in that farmhouse again.

"Who did you tell?" Derek snarled out his questions, demanding answers from the weeping figure at his side.

"N-no-nobody, I told nobody," the little man had sniveled, crying out when Derek fired his gun point blank into the chest of the only man left in the group of captives.

The other prisoners, all securely bound and gagged, stared with wide, tear-filled eyes as Derek continued with his questions before he turned his murderous gaze toward Noah.

"Go keep a lookout. If he's working with the Russians, they could be keeping patrols out watching over him. Last thing we need is to be surprised."

What Noah couldn't figure out was why he did what he was told at that moment. Derek was way out of line, and as messed up as his mind seemed to be, Noah was somehow aware that leaving and letting Derek murder those people wasn't the way he would normally have handled such a situation.

————

"So, what's the Dragon Lady got ya doin', kid?" Derek stood framed in the doorway, enjoying the look of surprise his sudden appearance caused.

"How did you get in here?" Noah asked. "Where's the guard that was out there?"

Derek frowned at the not so welcoming tone in Noah's voice, but the frown quickly turned to an indulgent smile.

"I told you, kid. I've got your back. Peterson has been put in her place, the guards have been sent back to wherever they came from, and you don't have to worry about the Dragon Lady anymore."

He limped slowly across the room, leaning heavily on a rolling walker while doing his best to hide the pain he was feeling with each step. When he got to the bed, he picked up the book Noah had just tossed aside.

"So, what's all this for?" he asked, reading the title before tossing it back onto the table.

He watched as Noah finally pulled himself together and managed to put a welcoming smile on his face. "Allison wants me to review agency protocol. How did you arrange to get her to call off the guard?"

"Good old Alex came through again. I'll introduce you to the old bastard one day, kid, when you've grown up a bit." He laughed and then carefully lowered himself into the chair that was next to the bed. "So what does the doctor say? How long till you're going to be back on your feet?"

"They haven't told me anything. I'm on this..." He showed Derek the IV lines in his hand. "For at least a couple more days, and they haven't let me get out of bed yet, so I would imagine it's going to be a while."

"Maybe so." Derek looked around the room before turning back to the young assassin with a grin on his face. "Hey, I've got a juicy bit of news for you, maybe even something that'll put a smile on that face." He leaned forward conspiratorially and said, "The Dragon Lady has cooled her breath down."

Noah gave him a puzzled look. "Her breath? What is that supposed to mean?"

"Jimmy Larsen has been putting his hostile environment training to good use," Derek chuckled. "He's been slipping into her bunk the past few nights, and she hasn't even breathed fire at him."

"Larsen and Allison?" Noah asked, his eyes going wide in surprise. In all the time he had known her, Allison had never seemed close to anyone outside the organization. He knew that a lot of people thought she and Donald Jefferson had something going on, but Noah had never seen anything to make him believe it was true.

"Yeah, good ol' Larsen the squid," Derek said. "He and the Dragon Lady are pretty damned cozy.""How do you—how did you find out?" Noah couldn't believe it. He imagined Larsen might have a way with the ladies, but Allison? That was a little bit hard to believe.

"Just keeping my eye on the signs. He was pretty tight with her out in the hall yesterday and when I made some comment, he got right up in my face." Derek let out a chuckle as he relived the scene in his mind. "It was kinda sweet really, watching Larsen jumping in, trying to defend his lady's honor. Ha, as if Peterson needs any defending. I doubt anybody else has ever had the guts to get that close to her. Hey, maybe that's why Larsen went there.

Maybe he likes living dangerously, or maybe she just likes guys who know how to follow orders blindly." He winked. "Bet she's got some black leather stashed away somewhere, don't you think?"

Noah sat staring off into space, and Derek was surprised at his lack of reaction. He watched the younger man for a moment, then leaned closer.

"So, just what did the Dragon Lady have to say to you?" Derek asked, changing the subject. "Did she tell you about the medals we're up for? Alex is pushing them, so we ought to get them in the next couple of days."

"Medals? But I thought..." Noah's eyes narrowed.

"What did you think, kid? You didn't think I was gonna come through for you? You need to have a little more confidence in me, I told you I've got it all under control. Sometime in the next couple of days, Peterson is going to have to stand up in front of everybody here and give a nice little speech about what a great job we did out there." He grinned. "Won't that be something? Her having to kiss our asses for once?"

Noah lay back and seemed to ignore him, and Derek's face took on an expression of anger, but the bags of fluid hanging on the pole caught his eye before he let the words burst out of his mouth. Antibiotics, no doubt, but they were probably laced with something for pain, as well. Poor kid was too dopey to understand what was going on, that had to be it.

He turned his attention to Noah again. "Hey, kid!" he said. "Pay attention when I'm talking to you, okay?" Noah's head slowly turned back to face him, and he went on. "Now, once we get the medals, I figure Peterson is going to ship you back to Neverland in a big hurry. Don't do anything until you hear from me, okay? I'm gonna pull some strings and get you out from under her. I think you've got a lot more potential than she gives you credit for, kid, potential to be one of the best agents the Company could ever get. We made a pretty good team in Germany, and I think we still have a lot we can do. Alex is setting me up with a new cover, some kind of diplomatic job, and I can get him to send you along as my sidekick, so we can work together when we have a real mission. You with me?" He watched the younger man, trying to be sure his words broke through Noah's obvious drug haze.

"Yeah, I get it," Noah said.

"Good. The new job is going to be in India, Delhi. I'll be heading out as soon as I can manage to walk without this godforsaken thing." He gave the wheeled walker a kick. "I can't get you transferred until after you've had your medical and psych evals and they declare you fit for duty, so when you get to that point, I'll get hold of Alex and get him started on snatching you out of there, okay?"

Noah nodded. He was slipping away again, his mind wandering. The more Derek talked, the less Noah wanted to hear what he had to say.

"I'm going back to my room," Derek said. "Just remember what I said. I don't think Peterson is done with you yet, so you be real careful what you say, and don't let yourself lose control when you talk to her." He leaned close again and lowered his voice. "Between you and me, soon as we're both out of here, I personally think the Dragon Lady has outlived her usefulness." He chuckled at his own comment and then got to his feet.

After making only a couple of slow, heavy steps toward the door, he turned back to Noah once more. "By the way," he said. "It might be time you tell the docs it doesn't hurt so bad anymore. Last thing we need is you to get hooked on those pain meds." He winked, then, and left the room.

James Larsen was sleeping with Allison Peterson? The idea had caught Noah completely by surprise; he would have never suspected that Allison would seek intimacy with a man like Larsen. Under normal circumstances, such an interesting little piece of gossip would have caused him to question whether he knew her as well as he thought he did. Larsen was the kind who probably had a girl in every port, so what the hell was he doing playing around with a woman like Allison? Allison wasn't ugly, but she was probably at least ten years older than the SEAL. There were probably plenty of younger, easier women on the base for him to mess around with.

In all the time he had known Allison Peterson, Noah had never heard a single believable rumor of her having a life outside of her job. How was it that, within a couple of days of arriving in Sigonella, she was sleeping with a man like Larsen?

Why would she go for a guy like him? Hell, why all of a sudden would she choose to have an affair with a Navy SEAL, of all people? Noah knew that a number of men in the intelligence world had tried to get close to Allison and failed, so why the hell was Larsen the one she would turn to?

The paranoia running loose in his mind caused him to leap to a simple conclusion: Allison was just using Larsen to solidify whatever it was she was planning to do to him. Larsen told her about what he had overheard from Noah, that he knew something really bad had happened in that farmhouse. It was Larsen who had gotten him to agree to turn his back on Derek Simpson. That had to be it, she was using Larsen to manipulate him into giving up Derek. Hell, she was most likely hoping that after a couple of weeks of working with the new recruits, he would crack and turn against Derek completely.

He lay back and let it all run through his mind. It seemed like it was all just some sort of a trick to make him do what they wanted. Hell, it even explained Derek talking about them getting the medals. Larsen had promised him that if he stayed away from Derek, if he accepted the job as a basic instructor, he wouldn't have to go through the farce of accepting the commendation. Larsen was fully aware that Noah absolutely did not want to accept a medal for something like what he and Derek had done.

They had probably figured that telling him he was going to get a medal would make him break, that he wouldn't be able to accept it. Larsen was supposed to make sure that plan got scuttled, but Derek seemed to think it was still right on schedule.

Noah sat upright, leaning his head forward as he rubbed his hands into his eyes. He was letting his paranoia take control. He had to slow down and think things through, look at everything calmly. The next time he saw Larsen, he was going to have to ask him point-blank about what was going on.

NINETEEN

ALLISON SAT AT HER DESK, HER FINGERS DRUMMING A monotonous tune as she listened to the audio feed during Derek's visit to Noah Wolf. She had turned on the computer as soon as she and Larsen had walked into her office a few minutes earlier and hit the play button. The two of them had sat silently as they heard the recorded conversation.

When it was over, Allison just looked at Larsen. The question in her eyes didn't need to be asked aloud.

"Well, I guess I have to admit that you were right about getting rid of the guards," Larsen said. "Derek definitely thinks he's the man in charge, for now." Larsen watched her carefully, prepared to make a fast retreat if Allison chose to let out any of the anger he could see building up in her face.

"But we haven't learned anything we didn't already know," she shot back, keeping the anger at bay. "Simpson is a pig, we already knew that, but Noah barely said a word. Do you think he knows I had Logan put ears in his room?"

Larsen shook his head. "No, Logan said Noah was out cold when he went in, and I believe him. That boy is doing his level best to impress you." He glanced over his shoulder toward the door, behind which Logan was sitting. "What is it with that kid, anyway? He's not one of your assassins, is he?"

Allison scoffed. "Logan? No. No, Logan came to me by accident. He was in a California prison for burglary, but not the average kind. He had gotten into a secure office on the thirty-fifth floor of a San Francisco financial institution and stole the security codes for their servers. That required coming down a rope from the roof on the outside of the building, drilling a hole through a sheet of glass without making a sound that could set off the alarm, using an air pistol to shoot plastic pellets at the security system keypad and punch in the correct code, then cutting another hole in the glass big enough to reach in and open the window. After that, it was just a matter of copying the access codes from a computer that some idiot forgot to lock down. By the time he was caught, he had created dozens of new accounts under fake identities he controlled, each of them with close to half a million dollars in it. I had gone there to recruit a potential assassin who happened to be his cellmate. The recruit agreed, but only on the condition that I take Logan along. When I found out what he had done, I figured he might come in handy."

Larsen chuckled. "You actually gave in to a recruit's demands?"

Allison shrugged. "Logan doesn't have what it takes to be an assassin, he is not a natural born killer. On the other hand, he pulled off that burglary when he was only eighteen years old. I can think of a number of ways he could be useful on a support team, can't you?"

"Hell," Larsen said, "I can think of ways to use him on my team." He turned back to Allison. "So," he said. "About Noah…"

Allison nodded and leaned back in her chair. "What did you make of the way Noah acted? He didn't tell him about taking the training job, or anything about you knowing any of the details about what happened at Reitner's place."

Larsen crossed his arms over his chest. "That actually has me a little worried," he said. "He's got some serious trust issues, right now, and he just found out that his boss is sleeping with the only one who seems to be on his side. That's got to make him wonder just how far he can trust either one of us, don't you think? I think I need to go talk to him, try to do some damage control. The last thing we need is for his paranoia to go into overdrive right now."

He had already made it to the door when she spoke again. "Larsen, remind him of the deal we offered. Make sure we keep him focused on that. And don't mention that his team is coming in. I'm hoping the surprise will help swing him over our direction."

———

NOAH WAS surprised when the door swung open again, not even fifteen minutes after Derek left. What did not surprise him was that Larsen was the one who came through it that time.

"Hey, Noah," Larsen said. "How you feeling?"

"I've been better," Noah said, trying to keep his face passive.

Larsen looked at him and let his eyes narrow a bit. "You look like something is bothering you," he said. "Something on your mind?"

Noah sat there silently for a moment, leaning back against the elevated mattress. A moment later, he indicated the door with his chin. "The guard who was standing outside is gone. I was wondering if something has changed about the deal we made," he said, carefully avoiding anything that might sound like an accusation.

"I thought you knew." Larsen raised an eyebrow. "I saw Derek in the hall. I thought he'd have told you. All the restrictions on both of you have been dropped."

Noah watched his face for a moment, then lowered his eyes.

"Yeah," he said. "Derek." The way he said the name told Larsen that he was feeling uncomfortable about being caught speaking to Simpson. "He said something I want to ask you about," Noah said, and then he paused before taking a deep breath and plunging ahead. "I was just curious, but how long have you known Allison? I mean, I get the feeling you two might know each other pretty well. Am I right?"

"I don't think that's anything you need to worry about, Noah," Larsen said nonchalantly, but before Noah could ask anything else, he held up a hand. "It's not a secret, I don't guess, just something we don't talk about lot. I've known Allison for about ten years, I guess. She was fairly new at her job as an analyst for the CIA, and I was attached and working on trying to find bin Laden. One of my reports apparently caught her attention, and she called me in the next time I was in D.C. because she wanted me to clarify some of the details. That was the first time we ever met, and I guess we've been friends ever since."

Noah watched him in silence for a moment, his face empty of any sign of emotion as he thought about what Larsen had said. They had known each other for ten years, but as far as Noah knew, Allison had never mentioned Larsen to anyone. He kept his face passive as he digested these facts, then looked at Larsen again.

"Derek said something about you and Allison maybe being more than just friends," he said.

"He told you I'm sleeping with her? Is that what you're trying to ask me?"

"Yeah," Noah said. "I guess it is." Now that the question was out in the open, he wanted to know the answer. He wanted to hear Larsen explain how he could be having an affair with Allison Peterson and not think it was worth mentioning.

"What goes on between us when we are off duty and in the privacy of our own quarters is nobody else's concern, Noah, and it has absolutely no effect on what I do when I'm on duty. Can you understand that?"

"I understand," Noah said, "but I think it makes me wonder how far I can trust you. I get the feeling now that maybe you and Allison might be working against me, trying to force me to turn on Derek if I want any chance of saving my career. That doesn't strike me as being open and transparent, you know? You and

Allison have every right to sleep with whoever you want, of course, but when I'm putting my life into somebody's hands, I like to know who I'm dealing with. If I can't trust you, I need to figure that out now."

"What would make you think you couldn't trust me?" Larsen asked, his face remaining passive. "Have you forgotten that I risked my own life to haul your ass out of that pit, when I would have been justified in simply calling in a drone strike to clean up the mess?"

Noah stared at him. A drone strike? It made sense; when a clandestine asset was compromised and captured, whenever retrieval was deemed to be too difficult, elimination was the fall-back answer. Larsen was correct. Considering that it was Larsen and one other man against God knows how many of the soldiers who had captured him, he would have been fully justified in calling for an elimination strike.

Larsen wasn't finished. "And just for the record, before you start trying to tell me that your boss just wants to get rid of you, how about remembering just how valuable you've been to her for the past three years? You were the best, do you remember that? Maybe you don't realize it, but an awful lot of people who get involved with Derek Simpson end up dead, one way or another. Once you were captured, she would have been within her rights to simply wash her hands of you, if that's what she wanted. Instead, she screamed at the State Department until they agreed to send my team in to get you."

Noah suddenly remembered Derek's comment about how Allison might have outlived her usefulness, but he wasn't sure whether he should mention it. Hell, he wasn't even sure what Derek might have meant by it. He had a hard time believing that Derek would try to get rid of her, but there had been rumors that other people who had gotten on his bad side found themselves dying under strange circumstances.

Larsen was still talking. "You want to know why you should trust me? Maybe you should ask yourself something else. Why in the world would you still trust Derek Simpson after knowing what he did to those people in that farmhouse? If that isn't enough to tell you who you can trust, then I don't know what to say, Noah!"

Larsen stood up and took a step back. Noah was silent, just staring at him as he thought about what Derek had said, and then added it to what Larsen had just told him.

"I'm sorry," he finally managed to say. "I let Derek... no, that's not true, it was all me. I do trust you, and I won't question you again." He looked away, overwhelmed by what the apology had meant to him.

"Okay then," Larsen said, suddenly acting as if nothing had happened. Noah flicked his eyes up as the table was moved back in front of him. "Then you need to get back to studying. Allison is arranging for you to get the notes and schedules from the training department later today. She's also looking at getting Derek moved over to the physical therapy clinic. It's all the way over on the other side of the medical complex, so maybe we can keep him out of your hair for a while."

Noah ran a hand over his face. He felt both physically and emotionally drained, and it wasn't even noon, yet. All he really wanted to do at that moment was close his eyes, but one look at Larsen's cool expression told him he was expected to get back to his books.

"Is this my punishment?" he asked quietly. "Am I being punished for what happened in Germany?"

"It's what you should have been doing in the first place instead of letting an asshole like Simpson fill your head up with crap." Larsen picked up the book on interrogation techniques and smiled over at the younger man. "Here, I'll help. There's a quiz in the back. Let's see how you do."

———

E & E Director Allison Peterson drummed her fingers on her desk top, her eyes narrowing as she listened to Derek Simpson giving Noah his own version of a pep talk on how to behave while he was being left unsupervised. She had already been over the recording several times, but it was only the last time that she let it play all the way to the end. Now she was trying to figure out if she had really heard what she thought she did.

SHE TOUCHED the computer screen and started the recording playing again. It was the very end of the recording, shortly before Simpson left the room.

"Between you and me, soon as we're both out of here, I personally think the Dragon Lady has outlived her usefulness."

She leaned forward and touched the screen again to stop the recording, her heart pounding against her ribs. *When I decided to record a meeting between Simpson and Noah,* she thought, *I confess I was hoping that it would give me a decent picture of Noah's state of mind, but I never expected this.*

Allison sat perfectly still for a moment, and then touched the intercom button on her desk.

"Michael," she called to Agent Logan. "Would you step in here for a moment?" She wasn't going to bother anyone else with this; Larsen had his hands full keeping Noah in line, and Alex Walker would probably ask Simpson what kind of assistance he needed to get the job done. If Allison was going to protect herself, it was going to have to be from within her own organization.

Derek Simpson was a threat, and she intended to deal with him in her own way, but there were other things she had to take care of at the moment.

"Yes, ma'am?" Logan asked.

"I need to get over to the airfield," Allison said. "And I'm going to need something big enough to bring back several people. Can you see if there is a van available?"

"Yes, ma'am," the young man said. He turned and was gone almost instantly, but was back less than two minutes later.

"Ma'am, I have a personnel transporter standing by outside for you right now. Shall I drive?"

Allison grinned at him. "Why not?" she said. "Let's go, I've got people due in almost any moment now."

The two of them left the building and Logan climbed behind the wheel of the modified Humvee. The machine looked like a giant station wagon, and Allison was pleased to see that the inside was laid out more like a small bus. There were the two seats up front, but the rest of them lined the walls of the main compartment.

The ride to the airfield took about fifteen minutes, and Allison was pleased to find that the shuttle plane was only just approaching for landing. She and Logan sat inside the small terminal building as the old twin-engine Beechcraft touched down and taxied up toward them. When the hatch popped open, she got up from her chair and walked outside, just in time to greet Nathan Parker as he climbed down the dancing steps.

"Allison," Parker said. "We are all here. Now, what the hell is going on?"

TWENTY

ALLISON WAITED UNTIL THE REST OF THE TEAM HAD climbed out of the aircraft, then led them all to the personnel carrier. Once they and their luggage were loaded inside, she climbed in and turned in her seat to look back at them.

"All right, here's the situation," she said. "You know that Noah was captured and was in pretty bad shape by the time we got him back. He had a massive concussion and a couple of broken ribs, probably from being kicked after he was down, and they removed a bullet from right beside his left kidney. He had lost some blood and had a nasty infection on the back of his head that resulted in having to remove the tissues. I'm afraid he's going to have a bit of a bald spot, but he can let his hair grow and keep it covered up for the most part." She held up a hand with her thumb and index finger making a small circle. "Don't panic, Sarah, it's only about the size of a quarter. Won't be that hard to hide."

Sarah gave her a wry grin. "He could lose all his hair, I'd still love him."

Allison's eyes softened. "I know that, sweetie," she said. "As for the rest of it, I'm afraid it gets worse. As I told you on the phone the other day, Noah seems to have recovered his emotions. In the few days we've had him back, he's been angry, he's been moping, cried like a baby a couple of times and displayed moments of being embarrassed and ashamed. This is not the Noah we know and love, not by a long shot. The trouble is that we don't know what caused this remission. One of my people thinks there might've been drugs involved, but the doctors assure me that there aren't any drugs that could cause something like this."

Parker glanced at her and she caught a barely noticeable wink, but didn't say anything.

"We've been doing our best to keep him busy, but there's another problem. The man he was working with on this mission is a CIA agent with a very bad reputation, a man who thinks nothing of killing just for sport. Noah seems to be under his influence to some degree, and we need Noah to give us a clear statement on what took place during their mission. Unfortunately, he's resisting that pretty stubbornly, almost like he's afraid to betray a friend. I have never seen him loyal to anyone outside your team, so I'm hoping that coming face-to-face with all of you again will help him to remember who he is."

"In that case," Sarah said, "I think there's something else you need to know." She gathered herself together and was about to speak when Allison held up a hand.

"That you are pregnant? Did you honestly think I wouldn't find out?" Allison smiled at her. "Don't worry, Sarah, I'm not going to chew you out or anything. Personally, I think it's wonderful, and I truly hope you're going to understand that I get to play grandma. I'm assuming Noah is aware?"

Sarah lowered her eyes. "No," she said. "I literally found out the morning you were sending him out on this mission. I didn't want to tell him before he left, because I didn't want him worrying about me. It almost slipped out, but I caught it in time."

Allison nodded. "Smart thinking," she said. "And to be honest, I'm not sure if this is going to be the right time to tell him. The only reason I know is because our doctors have orders to post all agents' medical records where I can get to them, and I had

Molly write a program that looks for certain words in them. One of those words is pregnancy, and it flagged after your last visit to the clinic."

"I was going to tell you," Sarah said. "I really was."

"She was," Jenny said. "Even if I had to drag her to your office. No way in the world we are going to let her go back out on another mission, not now."

"However," Renée said, "we also understand that this is a violation of the rules, so we're all a little worried about how you are going to handle it."

"How else can I handle it?" Allison asked. "Like I said, I want to be grandma. Do you people really think I didn't expect this to happen, once they got married? Your team has proven something that I once thought impossible, that agents like you can have normal relationships. Granted, you can only have them inside the organization, but at least you're able to love and be loved and have families. When I first started this organization, I didn't believe that was ever going to be possible at all."

"I still have my doubts," Parker said. "But let's get back to the subject at hand, can we? You said one of your people over here thinks Noah might have been drugged?"

"Yes, Lieutenant Commander Larsen. He said that there is something about the way Noah acted that made him wonder if Simpson, the CIA asshole I mentioned, might have slipped him a Mickey of some sort."

"I'm afraid I agree with your doctors," Parker said. "Highly unlikely that any normal drug could overturn his previous condition. However, there are some drugs that make people susceptible to suggestion. Has anyone tested his blood for those? Things like sodium pentothal, for instance?"

"I have no idea," Allison said. "I'm going to let you take charge of that part of the situation. What I really want right now is for all of you to get settled into the rooms I've arranged and be ready to go see Noah in about two hours."

Two hours of being quizzed by James Larsen on E & E interrogation techniques had left Noah Wolf's aching head reeling. While Larsen talked about the necessity of preparing where the interrogation was to take place and how to work on building up some trust with the subject, Noah suddenly found himself remembering how Jenny Lance handled interrogations. Her technique involved slicing various parts of the subject's body, and occasionally even removing certain important pieces, such as fingers or ears.

At least Larsen was gone, now. Noah was ready to relax, maybe even try to get a little more sleep, but then he heard voices in the hall outside. One of them sounded familiar, so he stopped and listened, and then the door opened.

Noah froze. Sarah, a smile on her beautiful face, stepped through the door and stopped to look at him. She took in the IV lines and the small bandage that still remained on the back of his head, but her smile never wavered. She stood where she was for almost half a minute, but then she rushed across the room and leaned over to throw her arms around him, just as he caught her in his own.

"Sarah?" he asked, his voice sounding incredulous. "What are you doing here?"

"Allison called," Sarah said, still holding him close. "You said you needed me, so I came. We all came, Noah, the whole team." She leaned back and looked into his eyes. "They're all outside in the hall, but I wanted a couple of minutes alone with you."

Noah broke into a huge smile, and Sarah suddenly felt a shiver of fear. She had never seen a genuine smile on his face before, at least not one this big. The best he had ever let out in the past was a small grin, but this was a smile of pure delight.

For him to wear a smile like that, there was definitely something very different about him. For the first time, she wondered if she would ever again see the Noah that she had fallen in love with.

"I'm so glad you did," he said. "God, you look wonderful."

"Well," she said, pulling herself together, "I wish I could say the same, but you look pretty rough. You got enough plumbing in you to make you look like a soda fountain."

Noah looked at her quizzically for a second, then grinned again. "Whatever," he said. "I'm just so glad to see you." Suddenly, his face clouded over. "Did Allison tell you? That I— well, that I'm kind of messed up right now?"

Sarah nodded. "I know. That's why I'm here, to help you get over it. Allison was hoping that maybe, if we work together, we can figure out what happened."

Noah shrugged. "I wish I knew," he said. "I haven't felt like myself in days. Even before I ended up here at the hospital, even back on the mission in Germany, there was something—I just wasn't right, you know?"

"Yeah, that's what I hear. Well, let's bring everybody else in so they can say hello, and then we can try to talk about it, okay?"

Noah nodded. "Yeah, that's okay," he said. He raised himself up a bit in the bed and Sarah was surprised when he tugged at his gown, trying to straighten it and make himself more presentable. She'd never seen him bother with such things before.

She walked over and opened the door, and the rest of the team stepped inside. One by one, they came over to the bed and either shook his hand or leaned over for a hug.

"Good to see you, boss," Neil said. "When are you going to get out of that bed so we can get back to work?"

Noah held up the arm with the IV line. "Soon as they unplug me," he said. "Trust me, I'm ready to go."

"I'll bet," Marco said. "I don't know about anybody else, but I hate being laid up in hospital. Seems like the hours last for days, and days last for weeks."

Noah chuckled. "Yeah, that pretty well fits."

The chuckle caught them all off-guard. They all looked at one another, confused. Neil recovered first.

"So," he said. "What's all this about you becoming an instructor?"

Noah grimaced. "You heard about that, did you? I guess Allison thinks I'm too messed up to go back out in the field for right now. She came up with the idea of having me work as an instructor for a while, I guess to see if I can pull myself together."

"You will," Sarah said. "You will, because there's no other choice."

Noah looked at her, and the thought went through his mind once again—should he fail—that he could end up in the potter's field.

He could not let that happen. Sarah deserved better from him.

———

The following morning, after a hot shower and a hearty breakfast, James Larsen made his way from the barracks over to Allison's temporary office, his mind going back over the previous evening. Having left Noah in the tender hands of his wife and the team, he had met Allison for a working dinner. The whole conversation had been about Derek and his not so subtle threat.

They had both ended up agreeing that to protect her reputation, they needed to let things cool down and, for her safety, given Derek's skills at assassination, she should probably take up residence off base. She arranged for a hotel room in the nearby town of Catania, and he returned to his own temporary quarters on the base.

Reaching her office, Larsen almost ran into Agent Logan on his way out of the door. "Hey, your boss in?" he asked before the trainee agent could run off on whatever errand he was being sent on.

"Yes," Logan replied with a smile. "As a matter of fact, she just asked me to go and find you. Good timing."

"Well, you found me." Larsen smiled back and stood clear of

the door frame so the young man could step back inside. Larsen watched the young agent disappear along the hallway with a grin on his face before he crossed the room to knock lightly on Allison's door.

"Come in, Larsen."

He stepped inside, instantly noticing the look of irritation on her face.

"How did you know it was me?"

"I recognized your knock." She smiled at him and then nodded at two identical black leather cases that were laying on her desk. "Look what arrived early this morning."

He crossed the room and picked up one of the two matching square cases. Opening the lid, he revealed a bronze cross against a pale blue silk ribbon.

"You gotta be kidding me," he said. "Walker went ahead with this?"

"Damn right he did." She looked him straight in the eye. "He expects me to pin those on Noah and Derek and tell them what a good job they did. Enough to make me want to puke."

Larsen put the award back into its box and closed the lid with a snap. "I can imagine," he said. "Does Noah know yet?"

"Of course not," she said. "And I'm damn sure not going to tell him, not right now." She gave him what he could only consider to be an evil smile. "That's going to be your job."

———

CLOSING the book he had been reading, Noah lay back against the pillows. He was waiting for Sarah and the others to come back and visit, but he knew they had been tired when they arrived, and probably more tired by the time they left his room at nearly midnight. They were probably sleeping in, while he had been roused for breakfast at six a.m.

Letting out a sigh, he pushed the table away. What he needed was some fresh air. He always thought better when he was on his feet. He hadn't been officially cleared to get out of bed, but the IV lines had finally been removed that morning, so there was nothing keeping him stuck in the bed. Besides, if they really wanted him to stay in bed, he was pretty sure somebody would have made it an order.

Carefully, he eased himself over to the edge so that his feet dangled inches off the floor. He stared down at his bare legs, realizing that all he had on was a hospital gown. Okay, so maybe he wouldn't venture out of his room quite yet.

Inching forward, he placed his feet flat on the floor, then rose up onto his feet and stood upright. He felt a bit lightheaded and the backs of his legs hurt, a lot, but it was nothing he couldn't handle. He was out of bed and he was going to show them he didn't need to wait for a doctor to tell him he was fine.

Smiling, he took one step away from the bed and the next thing he felt was when his forehead met the hard linoleum that covered the floor. He lay there stunned by what had just happened and then, as he tried to get back to his feet, a sudden wave of nausea overcame him and caused him to collapse back onto the floor.

He was stuck there, lying face down on the floor of his room with his head pounding. The pain at the moment was not from his original head wound, but from the fresh bump that was coming up on his forehead. Every effort he made to get up only made it worse, but there was no way he was going to call out for help. He heard footsteps outside in the corridor, but kept his mouth shut. If anyone were to find him like this, they'd never let him out of bed again. He made one more effort to get onto his hands and knees, unable to stifle a groan when he collapsed and the door to his room opened.

TWENTY-ONE

"Jeez, Noah! What the hell were you thinking? You okay, buddy?"

Noah looked up, seeing a set of laced combat jump boots, a pair of black pants and then, as he followed the clothing upwards, he found himself staring into the face of James Larsen.

"Yeah, well, I thought I was getting better," he muttered, a faint blush coloring his cheeks at being unable to get himself up off the floor.

"And what made you think you are ready to go for a stroll?" Larsen raised an eyebrow at him. Reaching for the remote beside the bed, he pressed on the call button.

"I just thought I'd go out and get some air." Noah glared when he realized Larsen had hit the call button for help. "You couldn't just give me a hand, help me get back in bed without ratting me out to the nurses?"

"Sorry, buddy, but you might have hurt yourself," Larsen said. He sat down on the edge of the bed while they waited for help to arrive.

It wasn't a long wait and as soon as the on call doctor and nurses arrived, he stood clear to let them work on getting Noah back into bed.

"Mr. Wolf, you're lucky you haven't managed to do any more damage to yourself," the doctor said. "Now, do me a favor and stay in bed or I will have to order restraints."

"Yeah, no problem," Noah said. "That's not something I want to do again today, anyway."

Once he was back in the bed and the staff was gone, Noah turned his angry glare onto the smiling Navy SEAL.

"What do you want now, Larsen?" he grumbled.

"I came to tell you the medals arrived this morning and that your boss is planning on handing them out tomorrow. She wants to get you and Simpson as far away from each other as she can, and as soon as possible. Are you ready to do this?"

"Do I have any choice?" Noah muttered darkly, gently probing at the fresh lump to his head and wincing.

"No, not really," Larsen agreed. "But you do have to decide whether you're going to accept the medal or not. Are you still planning to refuse it?"

"Damn right I am," Noah said. "I couldn't possibly accept it, not..."

"I understand, buddy," Larsen said. "Just remember that Simpson is going to be there. He's probably not going to handle it very well if you refuse."

"Think I give a shit?" Noah scowled, grimacing as he reached across to pick up one of the books on his table. "I already have to deal with this crap, I really don't care much what Derek Simpson thinks at the moment."

"That's what I want to hear," Larsen said with a grin. "Simpson is bad news, Noah. If you really want to do something right, you need to make an honest report about what happened on your latest mission. Let him face the music for what he did, rather than get some flashy promotion and be sent off to God knows where."

Noah frowned. "That's not easy," he said. "I know you don't really understand, but Derek—he's my friend, Larsen. It just doesn't feel right to turn on a friend."

"See, that's where you're messed up. Derek Simpson is nobody's friend, Noah. He's a killer..."

"What do you think I am?" Noah said. "I'm an assassin, Larsen, which means I'm a killer myself."

"Yes, you're an assassin," Larsen said. "According to Allison, you're the best she's ever seen, or you were. And one of the reasons for that is because you make it a point to avoid collateral damage whenever you can. Derek Simpson *is* collateral damage, by definition. You know that, you were there when it happened."

"That's not entirely true," Noah snapped. "Just so you know, Derek sent me away before he started killing those people..."

"What people is that?" Larsen said, jumping on Noah's slip. "What people did he kill, Noah? Look, we already know that Reitner and his entire family died, but he would have us believe that Reitner did it himself, blew up the house and killed his entire family just because he was afraid of people finding out he sold his country out to the Russians. Something about that doesn't ring true, Noah, but you are the only other person who knows what really happened. If you keep your mouth shut, he gets away with it. Is that what you want?"

"No," Noah said loudly. "No, I don't want him to get away with it, but I can't say for certain what happened after I left the house. I wasn't there, I wasn't there, you know what I mean?"

"I know that, Noah," Larsen replied softly. "But you have to remember that I heard the things you said when you were out of your head. You talked about children, and the teddy bear that kept looking at you. Maybe you weren't there when it happened, but you saw the aftermath, didn't you? Come on, Noah, come clean."

The anger was gone just as quickly as it had come and Noah slumped back in his bed, rubbing his eyes. It took a moment, but finally he looked up at Larsen again. "Just let me think about this, will you? I just need to think for a while."

"No problem, Noah," Larsen said. "I know your wife is

waiting to come see you, so I'll get out of here. You just—you send me word if you want to talk about this again."

Noah nodded, and Larsen turned and walked out of the room again. A moment later, the door opened and Sarah walked inside alone. She looked at Noah cautiously for a moment, then walked over and put a hand on his forehead.

"Hey, baby," she said. You doing okay?"

———

"AGENT SIMPSON, when I heard about your progress, I had to come down and see for myself," Allison said as she entered the physical therapy room.

Derek looked up, but continued with his workout. "I'm sure you did, sweetheart," he grunted. Releasing the dumbbells he had been lifting, he slowly raised himself into a sitting position.

Allison crossed her arms over her chest as she continued to look at him, his words on the recording still fresh in her mind.

"Once we're both in the clear and we have those awards, I think the Dragon Lady will have finally outlived her usefulness."

She hid her distaste behind a neutral expression. "I came to inform you the commendations arrived from D.C., and I've scheduled the ceremony for tomorrow afternoon. I've also arranged for your transfer to the envoy entourage in Delhi." She couldn't help a small smile at the look of surprise on his face. "It'll make it so much easier for you to keep up to date with the India situation."

She watched the play of emotions on his face. He was good, but he couldn't completely hide his anger. He wiped away the sweat beading on his forehead before making eye contact.

"The medals came in already?" He ground out the words from behind clenched teeth.

"Yes, you should thank Alex Walker for that," she answered calmly. "It seems that you must have made quite an impression on the CIA Director, because he was very eager to reward your good work."

Derek blinked at her. "It's always nice to be appreciated," he said as he got to his feet. He leaned on a wheeled walker, pushing it along so that she had to either back up or let him run over her toes.

"In that case, shouldn't you be writing your nice little speech about what a great job we did for the company, sweetie? If you'll excuse me, I've got things to do."

She pursed her lips as she watched him limp heavily across the room and out through the double doors. Apparently, he hadn't been aware that Walker had already approved and sent the medals.

Allison found that rather interesting.

———

DEREK REACHED his room and finally let his temper out, as he tossed the walker across the room. What the hell was Alex up to, sending those medals out so soon? He looked down at where his slippers lay under his bed. All his carefully laid plans were going to have to be moved up now. The Dragon Lady, James Larsen and now director of the CIA— Derek would end up getting rid of them all, even Alex, if he ever tried thinking for himself again. How dare he do anything without checking with Derek first?

With an effort, Derek managed to walk over to his bed and sat down heavily. He looked at his slippers again. Those few pills he had stashed away weren't going to be enough. *I'm going to need to get into the pharmacy. I need something with more power that's not going to turn up on a routine tox screen.*

Laying himself back on the bed, he closed his eyes and started to plot.

Getting into the pharmacy wasn't going to problem, but he wouldn't have the time to build up his strength. That was going to be the only real problem; he was going to have to recruit some help again, but he wasn't going to mess with some insipid little nurse again. He needed somebody tough enough to get the job done, but somebody who would keep his mouth shut about it afterward, and that wouldn't be easy to find on a naval base.

The anger slowly slipped away and the corners of his lips curved into a smile at the sudden thought of all the sharp implements he could get his hands on. If the pharmacy was going to be out of bounds for now, maybe he could take advantage of another form of attack. Hospitals presented him with so many wonderful opportunities, but while thinking about any particular method of assassination should have lightened his mood, he knew that a sudden onslaught of heart attacks or a number of throats being cut all at the same time would bring too much unwanted attention his way.

Damn Walker for trying to think for himself, and damn that bitch Peterson for...

His eyes snapped open and a curse escaped from between his tightly clenched lips. Idiot! He sat upright, cursing again when he pulled at his stitches. Amateur! When he had entered his room, he had been so furious at Walker for messing up his carefully laid out plans that in his rage, he had missed a few very interesting changes to his room.

Hanging up on the outside of his closet was a cheap black suit jacket and a white cotton shirt. Underneath, folded neatly on a chair, were the matching suit pants and a set of underwear. The clothes alerted him to the fact that somebody from the Company had been in his room and he had a very good idea who it had been.

Peterson, the Dragon Lady herself, had undoubtedly brought the suit in and hung it up. It would give her the chance to take a look inside his room, and she would never be able to pass up such an opportunity.

From his position sitting up on the bed, he scanned the room with a professional eye. At first glance, the positioning of his things looked exactly the way he had left them, but searching rooms was something he did pretty often, so he was fully aware of what signs to look for to determine if somebody had done it to him. Now that he was alert, he could see there were tiny clues all about the room that only somebody with training like his would ever notice.

His eyes fell to where his slippers lay on the floor, the toes just peeking out from under the bed. Carefully, he reached down and picked them up. Looking closely at the stitching and feeling around with his sensitive fingers, he allowed himself a small smile of relief. Maybe Peterson wasn't as smart as she thought she was. The pills were still where he had put them.

That feeling of relief didn't last long, however. He had survived so long in a business with a higher than average mortality rate because of his highly developed sense of self preservation and paranoia. He dropped the slippers back to the floor and focused his attention on the phone and the electrical outlet beside the bed. He ran through his meeting with Allison, picking through her little speech, looking for clues to her real meaning.

"I came to inform you the commendations arrived from D.C. and I've scheduled the ceremony for tomorrow afternoon."

"You should thank Alex Walker. He was very eager to reward your good work."

Scowling, he picked up the handset and looked closely at the mouthpiece. Removing the cap to get to the microphone, he found the micro transmitter hidden inside. He nodded thoughtfully, then put the handset back together and replaced it on its cradle.

She had expected him to call Walker, so she must be at least somewhat aware of their relationship. He worried his lower lip with his teeth for a moment. As far as he was concerned, this gave him even more reason to send the bitch to an early grave, but first he was going to have to find out how much she knew and just who she had told.

Picking up his slippers again, he opened the lining and dug out the pills. With a sigh, he got up and hobbled to the bathroom, then took one last, lingering look at the pills before flushing them down the toilet. If he was going to spend some quiet time questioning Peterson, it was going to have to wait until he was fit enough to be able to control her.

He got the walker and used it to get back to the bed. Lying back on the covers, he had another thought. He might as well try to come up with some kind of terminal accident for Larsen while he was at it.

————

"Hey, Noah," Neil said as he entered the room. Sarah was sitting beside Noah on the bed, smiling as she held his hand. "You seem to be doing a little better today. Am I right about that?"

"Hey, Neil. Yeah, I guess so." He glanced up at Sarah. "Something about having Sarah with me makes the world seem a little better."

"Oh, nice save, there, Noah," Jenny said. "Good thing you gave credit to Sarah, I might have to kick your butt."

Noah grinned at her. "We wouldn't want that, now, would we?"

"No, you wouldn't," Neil said. "Trust me."

"Wouldn't what?" Marco asked as he and Renée entered the room. "What is it we don't want?"

"Noah doesn't want me to kick his ass," Jenny said.

"Oh, is that the incentive we're using today?" Marco asked.

Noah looked at him. "Incentive? Incentive for what?"

TWENTY-TWO

Marco shrugged. "Incentive to get you to pull yourself together and get back to being your lovable old robotic self," he said. "I figured Jenny was threatening you or something."

Noah's face suddenly looked sour. "I wish there was a way she could do it," he said. "It's really weird, I know I'm not acting normal, because I'm acting too normal. This just isn't me, but I have no idea what happened to make me this way."

———

In Allison's office, she and Nathan Parker were listening to the audio feed from Noah's room. The banter between Noah and his team seemed strained, but the obvious affection they held for one another was present.

"Any ideas, Nathan?" Allison asked.

The old psychiatrist looked at the computer screen, even though it only showed the squiggly line of the audio feed. "It looks to me like he's had some sort of breakdown," he said. "The trouble is that, after everything he's done and been through, I can't imagine what could possibly have caused it. Allison, if I didn't know better, I'd say he has at least partially regressed to his childhood. There is almost an innocence in the way he talks, almost as if he's the little boy who saw his daddy kill his mother, rather than the grown man we have all come to know."

Allison cocked her head to the side and looked at him. "You know, that does make a little sense," she said. "It was after that happened that he suddenly became emotionless, right? Could it be that something triggered his mind to go back to just before that happened?"

Parker shrugged. "It's certainly possible. If I had some idea what the trigger was, we might be able to figure out some way to remove it, undo the damage. Any thoughts?"

Allison reached over and picked up a file folder. "This is the transcript of my interview with James Larsen, the Navy SEAL to lead the team that brought him in. He says Noah was talking a lot, especially when he was not quite awake. You can scan through that, see if you notice anything."

Parker took the file and opened it up, slowly turning the pages as he read through them. Allison went back to listening to the conversation in the hospital room, but it was only a few minutes later that Parker suddenly sat forward and slapped the desk.

"That's it," he said. "That's got to be it."

"What?" Allison asked. "Did you find something?"

"Yes, I did," Parker said. "And you can be extremely grateful for the fact that I have not managed to develop memory troubles in my old age. Remember when you first brought Noah in? Our initial interview? I got him to talk a lot about his life, including his childhood before the incident that had such an impact on him. There was one thing he mentioned, something that seemed so insignificant I never thought about it again, but now it's making sense in this situation."

Allison stared at him. "Nathan Parker, if you don't tell me what the hell you're talking about, I'm going to rip your head off."

Parker pointed at a line in the page in front of him. "This," he said. "Apparently, he kept talking about a teddy bear that was looking at him."

Allison nodded. "Yes, I saw that," she said. "Are you telling me that it's somehow relevant?"

"Damn right it is," Parker said. "When Noah's parents died, there was blood everywhere. One of the police officers who came to the scene him took away his favorite toy because it was covered in his mother's blood. Care to guess what it was?"

Allison's eyes went wide. "Oh, my God," she said softly. "A teddy bear?"

"Exactly," Parker said. "It didn't dawn on me at the time, but that teddy bear had to have had serious emotional importance to the little boy for him to still remember it after so many other traumatic events in his life failed to have any significant effect on him. I would bet you just about anything, including my pension, that the teddy bear he saw in that farmhouse reminded him of the one he lost that day. For a man with the disorder he was diagnosed with, that could easily trigger regression back to the moment before his original teddy bear became tainted with blood. That would be the moment before his mother died, and the moments before his emotions were shoved so far back into his psyche that he can't even find them anymore."

———

"THIS IS ALEX," Walker's voice said through the phone. "Derek?"

"Yep," Derek said, "it's me, Alex. Listen, I was calling to thank you for getting the commendations put through so quickly."

"Why, it's my pleasure," Walker said. "I was going to call you shortly anyway, to tell you that I've made the arrangements for your promotion and posting. Everything is all set, you will be leaving for India as soon as the doctors release you there."

"No, that's good, that's good," Derek said. "I may have run into a little bit of a problem in here, though. You know. Allison

Peterson has been causing me a bit of grief. I was just kind of wondering, what's the general sentiment on Capitol Hill about her lately?"

Walker was quiet for a moment. "Allison is a valued colleague," he said cautiously. "It would be a terrible shame if anything were to happen to her. Her organization would probably founder completely, without her at the head."

Derek grinned. Walker understood exactly what he was saying, and had given his tacit blessing.

"Well, we wouldn't want anything like that to happen," he said. "Of course, she should know better than to come out to dangerous areas like this. I mean, sure, we're actually on a naval base within one of our allied countries, but things can happen, you know what I mean?"

"I'm afraid I do," Walker said. "Dangerous place, dangerous place, indeed. I'm sure you'll do everything possible to make sure to keep yourself out of danger, right?"

"Of course, Alex," Derek said. "Don't I always?"

"It makes me very glad to hear it," Walker said. "Just be as circumspect as you can, please? The last thing we would need is for anything untoward to happen, and splash any mud back on the Company."

"Absolutely," Derek said.

The two of them ended the call a moment later, and Derek got to his feet with the help of the rolling walker. He leaned on the handlebars as he pushed it along, a couple of fingers hooked into each of the brakes as he made his way out of the room and into the hall.

There were a number of Italian personnel on the base, and many of them carried sidearms. The Beretta 92FS was a fine piece of personal armament, a nine millimeter semiautomatic pistol that was highly effective in close quarters combat, and surprisingly quieter than most similar weapons. Eric knew that some of the security guards for the hospital were among those personnel, and that they had rooms on the top floor of the building. He made sure nobody was looking and took the elevator up, ready to make the excuse that he had meant to go to the physical therapy room on the fifth floor if anyone asked why he was up there.

Surprisingly, the eighth floor was completely deserted when the elevator opened. It took him less than a minute to make his way into the first room he came to, quietly picking the lock and stepping inside. He left the walker just inside the doorway, leaning against the wall as he made his way into the darkened room.

"What..." The voice came from the bedroom, and Derek cursed himself for choosing a room where one of the night guards was getting some sleep.

Before the man could react, Derek steeled himself for the pain in his leg and launched himself through the doorway. The heel of his hand struck the base of the Italian soldier's nose, and it was all over. The man was dead instantly, the bridge of his nose driven directly into the frontal lobe of his brain, some of the bone even making it into the hippocampus. The body twitched a couple of times and lay still as blood began to run from the nostrils.

Derek shook his head. *Sloppy,* he told himself. *That was sloppy, Derek. Now we have to clean up another mess.*

He got to his feet and made a quick search of the bedroom, finding the pistol he was looking for in the nightstand. Luckily, the man had been sleeping alone. If he hadn't been, the situation could've gotten out of hand. Derek might have been exposed, which would have angered Alex Walker.

"Screw Walker," Derek said aloud. He looked at the bloodied bed and thought about how to make sure no one could connect the murder to him, but the only solution was going to be to destroy any trace of the DNA he might've left behind.

He made his way to the kitchen and set a pot of water on the stove, then laid a towel on the counter so that part of it was directly adjacent to the burner. He turned it on and quickly made his way out of the apartment, thankful to see that no one was in the hallway. He got into the elevator and took it down to the main floor, confident that the building's fire suppression system would be able to control the blaze that was going to break out upstairs before it did any serious damage to the hospital sections.

Now, all he had to do was find Larsen and his girlfriend together, someplace where there wouldn't be any witnesses.

———

Noah was sitting up on the bed, and had even made it to the bathroom with Marco helping him. He declared that to be one of the high points of his life so far, just to be able to escape the confines of the hospital bed for a few minutes.

"I can imagine," Marco said. "I told you, I hate hospitals. Next time I get shot, you could put me in a trash bag and set me out at the curb. I'm not worried about getting patched up, staying in the hospital is too much like being dead, anyway."

Renée slapped him on the shoulder. "Knock it off," she said. "I'm not ready to give you up just yet."

Marco started to say something else, but then the door opened and Doctor Parker walked in.

"Doc," Noah said with a smile. "They didn't tell me you were here. It's good to see you."

Parker's eyebrows rose. "I haven't heard that very many times in my life," he said. "I need to speak with Noah alone for a few minutes," he continued. "Would all of you mind waiting somewhere else for a little while? It's close enough to lunchtime, if you want to go down to the cafeteria, get yourselves something to eat."

"Lunch, yeah," Neil said. "That's a great idea. Come on, everyone, let's go get some lunch."

Sarah looked irritated, but she leaned down and kissed Noah on the cheek. "I'll be back as soon as I can," she said. "I love you, Noah."

"Love you too," Noah said. "Go on, they'll be bringing my lunch in a few minutes, anyway."

The five of them left the room, and Noah was alone with

Parker. He looked up at the old psychiatrist and the smile disappeared off his face.

"You're not here to wish me luck," Noah said. "You're here to figure out what's wrong with me, right?"

"I'm afraid that's true, Noah," Parker said. "And I'm delighted to say that I think I have done exactly that."

Noah scowled, and his bottom lip stuck out. "And what is it?" he asked. "What made me like this? I can't even manage to think clearly, can you believe that?"

"Oh, I can believe it quite easily," Parker said. "Noah, do you remember the day your parents died?"

Noah's eyes closed suddenly. "Of course I do," he said. "How could anybody forget something like that?"

"I want to talk to you for a moment about what happened just before they died. Can you remember the last few moments, before everything got so bad?"

Noah was quiet for a couple of seconds, but then he nodded. "Of course I do," he said. "I had been upstairs doing my homework, and my parents were downstairs fighting. It went on so long I decided to go see what was happening, because I was worried that Mom might end up bruised again." He swallowed hard. "My dad was yelling about money, but he couldn't find where he said my mother had hidden it, but she kept insisting there wasn't any money. I remember he had a gun in his hand, and he pointed at his head, and my mother yelled at him to stop..."

"Go on," Parker said. "Tell me what you were doing at that moment, can you do that?"

"I—I was standing just outside the door of the room, and I remember I held my teddy bear as tight as I could. For just a second, I thought my dad was going to shoot himself, but then he turned and pointed the gun at my mother and..."

"Go on, Noah," Parker said. "What happened next?"

Noah's eyes opened and he looked directly into Parker's own. "My father pulled the trigger," he said. "The gun went off and the bullet hit my mother between the eyes. Her head blew apart as I watched, and the blood and gore came flying my direction. I was so startled that I yelled, and that's when my dad saw me. He looked at me for just a moment, then pointed the gun at his own head and pulled the trigger again."

Parker nodded. "And how did you feel at that moment?"

Noah cocked his head slightly to the left. "Feel? I didn't feel anything," he said. "They were dead, I realized that, and I had a little bit of blood on me, but most of it hit the bear. I had dropped it when the police came, and I remember that I went to pick it up, but the female officer that came in to watch me took it away."

Parker nodded again. "Tell me something, Noah," he said. "When did you see that teddy bear again?"

"The teddy bear? I never..." He suddenly trailed off, and his eyes rose toward the ceiling. A moment later, he looked at Parker again. "Reitner's place," he said. "There was a teddy bear there, it was just like mine. This little kid was holding it, a little kid who was dead, and I remember thinking that it was looking at me, blaming me."

Parker stared at him for a moment, then leaned close and looked into his eyes.

"How are you feeling right now, Noah?"

Noah stared into his eyes. "I'm not feeling anything," he said. "Nothing at all. And that tells me that it was the teddy bear that caused the problem, am I right?"

"Undoubtedly," Parker said, nodding. "For whatever reason, it took you back to that moment before your mother died, and you've been trapped in some sort of mental loop to catch you feeling like that seven-year-old boy. He had all the emotions that you lacked, Noah, so suddenly you felt them all again."

Noah nodded. "I understand," he said. "It all makes sense, now. That's why I was doing whatever Simpson told me to do, it's why I was so determined to protect him."

Parker nodded once more. "Indeed," he said. "I'm guessing you saw the teddy bear before the child was killed, and it triggered a flashback. When everything happened so quickly, you got stuck in that flashback, which meant that Agent Simpson was suddenly your male authority figure. He took the place of your father, whom you would naturally want to protect." He leaned closer toward Noah. "But, now I think you can see that his actions constitute a pretty serious problem, can't you?"

"I can," Noah said. "He's a psychopath, and is using his position as a CIA agent to cover himself while he seeks out his victims. He doesn't kill because he has to, he kills because he enjoys it."

Parker started to speak, but Noah's eyes suddenly went wide. "Allison is in danger," he said. "Simpson told me that she has outlived her usefulness. I'm fairly certain he intends to try to kill her, probably at any moment now."

TWENTY-THREE

PARKER SHOUTED FOR MARCO, WHO CAME RUSHING IN. "Doc?" he demanded. "What's going on?"

Noah answered. "Marco, Agent Derek Simpson is planning to kill Allison Peterson. I want you to get to her as quickly as you can, warn her that he will be coming. Sarah and the rest of the team need to go back to their quarters, but arm yourselves, all of you. If he comes near any of you, take him down. He's a psychopathic murderer, and is on a rampage."

"You got it, boss," Marco said. He turned and headed out the door instantly, and Noah could hear him relaying the orders to the rest of the team. He also heard Sarah refusing to leave, but Neil and Jenny took her by the arms and dragged her out of the building.

———

IN HER OFFICE, Allison's eyes went wide. She had suspected Derek was going to try to kill her, but Noah seemed to think it was going to happen almost immediately. She reached across the desk for her phone, but was interrupted when the sound of a fire alarm suddenly blared through the computer speakers.

Michael Logan stuck his head in the room. "Ma'am, there's a fire at the hospital," he said. "It seems to be on the top floor. The base fire department is responding, and the commander's office says the fire should be contained to a small part of the top floor. They'll be watching the situation, in case they need to evacuate the hospital."

Allison shook her head. "Good heavens," she said. "Logan, are you armed?"

"Of course I am, ma'am," he said. "Why? Is there something wrong?"

"I've just been advised that Agent Simpson may be planning to pay me a visit, the kind of visit that I won't be returning from," she said. "Do me a favor, find Jim Larsen and get word to him to get over here. And whatever you do, Logan, don't try to take Simpson on yourself. He's a trained killer, as deadly as they come. I'm not ready to lose you just yet, got that?"

His eyes wide, Logan nodded. "Got it, ma'am," he said. He vanished back out the door and she heard him on his phone a moment later, trying to locate Larsen.

———

JAMES LARSEN WAS at the hospital, visiting the wounded members of his team. All of them were recovering, and better than anyone had expected, but the sound of the fire alarm wiped the smile off his face. He hurried out of the room and to the nurses' station, demanding to know what was happening.

"We're not entirely sure, sir," the nurse said. "All I know at the moment is that there's a fire on the top floor, but the sprinklers are working and the fire department is on the way. I don't think there's any danger to the patients, at least not at this moment. I know that we aren't under any orders to evacuate."

"How the hell could a fire start on the top floor?" Larsen asked. He wasn't really expecting a response, but he got one anyway.

"It's an old building, sir," the nurse said. "Probably an electrical fire or something."

"Or something," Larsen said. On a hunch, he turned and headed toward Simpson's room, which was now on the other side of the building. He found it with no trouble, but Simpson wasn't there. An itch began at the back of his skull, and he was trying to figure out what it meant when his cell phone went off in his pocket. He snatched it out and put it to his ear. "Larsen," he said.

"Commander Larsen, this is Agent Logan, from Director Peterson's office. She would like to see you at your earliest convenience."

"Yeah, I'll bet she would," Larsen said. "Tell her I'll be there in a minute, there's somebody I need to find, first."

"Would that be Agent Simpson? Commander, that's the reason she asked me to call. Apparently, she just got the word that Agent Simpson may be planning to kill her, like now."

Larsen's eyes went wide, and he turned and ran back the way he had come. "Tell her I'm on the way," he said, then cut off the call and dropped the phone into his pocket. As he ran, he cursed himself for not having a weapon with him, but it wasn't usually necessary when he was on base.

———

NOAH WAS CLIMBING out of the bed, and nothing Parker could say was going to make him stay there. With his hospital Johnny flapping behind him, he forced himself to hurry out the door and held onto the rail along the hallway wall as he hurried toward the front entrance of the building.

Parker caught up a moment later. "Noah, where do you think you're going?"

"I gotta get Allison," Noah said. "If Derek gets to her, he will kill her."

"And you're in no shape to do anything about it," Parker said.

"I'll sound the alarm, he won't be able to hide well enough to get away."

"The hell he won't," Noah said. "Derek Simpson is a master of disguise, as well as at infil- and exfiltration. The only way we're going to catch him is to be waiting when he gets to her."

"Maybe so, but if he sees you..."

"He won't think anything about it," Noah said. "He still thinks he's got me under control, and I'm going to keep him believing that."

"How do you plan to achieve that?" Parker asked, exasperated, but then he looked at Noah's face.

Tears were streaming down his cheeks, and Noah looked like a terrified child. "Camouflage, Doc," Noah said softly. "Derek probably knows that I was regressed to my childhood, so this is going to look natural to him."

Parker couldn't keep up, and stopped to lean against the wall. Noah kept going, rushing right out the door, hospital gown still flapping and exposing his ass as he hurried along.

He was calling for Allison as he jogged as quickly as he could manage.

———

THE FIRE WAS PLAYING RIGHT into Derek's plans. When the alarm went off, he had been hiding just down the hall from where Larsen was visiting his teammate, and he had seen the SEAL hurry out of the room. He hadn't been able to keep up, but a moment later, he had spotted Larsen again, heading for the front door. Derek broke into a smile as he realized the man was running to try to protect Allison from whatever might be happening.

"Dumb ass," he muttered. "The fire is at the hospital, not at her office, but you rush on over there. That way I've got both of you where I want you."

He pushed the rolling walker along, making his way out the door only a moment after Larsen. It was only a few hundred yards to the building where Allison had her temporary office, and he was moving along at a pretty good clip for a crippled guy.

He got to the building a couple of minutes after Larsen, but he didn't go through the front door. He had been to this base before, and knew this building fairly well. There was another entrance at the back, one that was normally used only by maintenance personnel. He hurried around the building, pushing the walker along and doing his best to look like one of the old men who lived with some of their family members on the base.

It must have been working, because nobody was paying attention to him. He got to the back of the building and slipped through the door without anybody noticing, and then stopped to plan how he was going to get to Allison. Her office was only a short distance away, but it had only one entry. He knew that kid, Logan, was going to be sitting in the anteroom, but he wouldn't be much of a problem. It was Larsen who was likely to put up a fight, and Derek was ready for him.

There it was, Allison's office. Derek moved as quietly as he could toward the door, then pushed it open gently. Logan wasn't at his desk, for some reason, but that only helped Derek accomplish his goals. He slipped inside and shut the door behind them, twisting the lock to make sure he wouldn't be interrupted.

He could hear Larsen and Allison through the door into her office, and she was saying something about how Derek was coming to kill her.

Derek grinned. So much the better, if she knew it was coming. There was nothing like seeing the terror in their eyes as you pulled the trigger.

———

NOAH HAD to ask someone where Allison's office was, since he hadn't even been out of the hospital until now, but the young sailor was happy to give him directions. It wasn't that far, and

Noah was moving as quickly as he could even as people were pointing and laughing.

Somebody had called the base Shore Patrol, and one of their officers caught up to him when he was only a dozen yards from the building.

"Sir," the sailor said, "I'm going to have to ask you to come with me."

Noah looked at him for a second, his tear stained face causing the man to lean back in surprise, and then punched him quickly on the point of the jaw. The sailor dropped like a sack of potatoes, and Noah bent down to snatch his service sidearm from its holster, then continued on his way. A dozen onlookers were staring, but when they saw the crazy man in the hospital gown with a pistol in his hand, they all decided they had somewhere else they needed to be.

Noah shoved his way through the front door of the building and started looking for Allison's office. He knew it wasn't likely to have her name on the door, but it was bound to say something about E & E. The building directory didn't help, so he just kept going from door to door, trying each one and glancing inside. A number of secretaries and administrative aides looked up startled, but he simply shut those doors and went on to the next.

And then he found one that was locked. His gut instinct told him this was Allison's office, and that Derek was probably already inside. He looked at the lock on the door for a moment, then leaned back against the opposite wall of the hallway and kicked with everything he had.

It wasn't enough. He had been lying down so long that he was feeling weak, and he just didn't have the energy to put into the kick. He thought for a brief moment about trying to crash through with his shoulder, but then only shook his head. He aimed the pistol at the doorknob and pulled the trigger, and the forty-five caliber slug blew the lock completely out of the door.

The door flew open, and Noah found himself staring into an

empty room. There was another door across the way, and he hurried to it, then stopped and put his ear against it.

———

"You're not going to get away with this, you know," Allison said. "As you can tell, we knew you were coming. Even if you managed to kill us both, the word is already out about you."

Derek smirked at her. "And you think that worries me? Do you know how many times Alex Walker has had to pull my fat out of the fire? He knew I was coming after you, and he told me to make sure I was safe, but he can't afford for me to get caught. He'll do whatever he has to do to cover it up."

He raised the pistol and pointed it directly at Allison's face; that was when all hell broke loose. The door behind him suddenly flew open, and he heard Noah's voice.

"Put down your weapon, Derek," Noah said.

Derek froze where he stood, not letting his aim waver for a second. There was something about Noah's voice, something different, and it took him a second to put his finger on it.

Yeah, that was it. It sounded the way he'd sounded when they first met, nearly two weeks earlier. He didn't know exactly how Noah had regressed to his childhood during the mission, but he could tell that it was over.

"Be smart, Noah," he said over his shoulder. "If we don't take her out, she's going to let you be burned. If the oversight committee ever finds out what we really did on this last mission, it's all..."

"You mean, what you did," Noah said. "I was compromised, and you took advantage of my condition. You murdered an incredible number of innocent people, Derek, and then you basically brainwashed me to cover it up for you. Sorry, but I can't continue with that. Put your weapon down, or I'm going to kill you."

"My finger is on the trigger," Derek said, "and the barrel is aimed directly at the Dragon Lady's face. You shoot me now, there's a pretty good chance I'm going to squeeze the trigger out of pure reflex, even if you take out the brain. Unless you're willing to risk that, put your weapon down."

"That's not going to work," Allison said. "Noah is back, dammit, and there's nothing you can use to blackmail him into giving up to you now. Go ahead and shoot me if you want, but that won't stop him."

"If that were true," Derek said, "I'd be dead already. He doesn't want to risk that reflex trigger squeeze." He licked his lips. "Noah, I'll tell you what," he said. "You put your weapon down, and I will turn and walk out of here. I won't hurt Peterson, or anyone else. We'll pretend this never happened, and let Alex clean up the mess however he wants to."

"No way, Derek," Noah said. "After what you did in that farmhouse, I am not going to let you walk away. You will either face justice for your crimes, or I will put you down here and now."

Derek gritted his teeth, and a low growl escaped his throat. "Well, in that case," he said, "I might as well have my last bit of fun."

He pushed his pistol forward and squeezed the trigger, but James Larsen had expected it and was already moving, his body slamming backward into Allison as the bullet caught him in the chest. At such close range, the nine millimeter slug went all the way through, but it lost a lot of momentum piercing his breast-bone. By the time it hit Allison, it was deflected upward and merely shattered her collarbone as it tore into her shoulder.

Noah fired, and Derek Simpson ceased to exist.

EPILOGUE

It took almost six hours for the Shore Patrol and NCIS to figure out what happened, and another three hours for all of the phone calls back to D.C. Because both Allison and Noah had heard Derek Simpson brag about how Alex Walker would cover for him over murdering Allison, the President of the United States decided to remove Walker as Director of the CIA. His deputy, a woman named Linda Myers, was appointed as interim director and Walker was ordered to undergo federal investigation.

Over the next several days, Noah underwent intense questioning about the mission to Germany, and the State Department used his responses to build a cover story. Derek Simpson, they made clear, was a rogue agent who had abandoned his job at the CIA a year earlier, entering the private sector as an intelligence broker. The German government, with doubt clamped firmly between their teeth, accepted the story and U.S.-German relations began the long road to recovery.

Noah and his entire team attended the military funeral of Lieutenant Commander James Larsen two weeks later, at Arlington. Nobody knew exactly who they were, but it was clear that they were VIPs who were not to be disturbed. Allison stood with them, dressed in black.

With that, the situation was finally concluded. As they flew back to Neverland together on the Gulfstream, Allison turned to Noah.

"Has she told you yet?" she asked.

Noah looked at her. "Has who told me what?"

Allison turned her eyes towards Sarah and gave her a mock look of anger. "Now, Missy, or I'm going to do it myself."

Sarah bit her bottom lip, then turned to her husband, who was sitting beside her.

"I didn't want to tell you before you went on this mission," she said, "and then everything was so screwed up by the time we got to Italy, I didn't want to tell you then. After that, you were under so much pressure to handle the investigation into Simpson, so there didn't seem to be a good time, but I guess this is probably as good as it's going to get."

Noah was looking at her, confusion evident on his face. When she suddenly smiled, the confusion lifted.

"You're pregnant?" he asked.

The smile disappeared, replaced with a glare. "You can't ever let me surprise you with anything, can you?" she asked. "I was doing my best to surprise you. You saw that, right, Allison? I tried to surprise him, didn't I?"

"You tried," Allison said with a chuckle. "On the other hand, he's Noah Wolf."

Sarah huffed once more, then turned to Noah again. "Yes, I'm pregnant. We are going to have a baby."

Noah stared at her for a moment, then turned to Allison. "And what is this going to mean for the team?"

"It's going to mean you get another transportation specialist," Allison said, "because there is no way I'm going to let my grand-child, or her mother, go out on any more missions. I actually thought about retiring all of you, but I'm afraid that simply isn't possible. No matter what else is true, Noah, you are still the best I've got."

Noah nodded. "I understand," he said. "Thank you, because I really don't want Sarah going out on any more missions."

"Well, we are agreed on that," Allison said. "And, now that that's out of the way, I have one more thing to tell you. I think you all need to go back to the manor house in England for a while, take a couple of months off. And if you don't mind, I think I'm going to come along."

Don't miss DEEP ALLEGIANCE. The riveting sequel in the Noah Wolf Thriller series.

Scan the QR code below to purchase DEEP ALLEGIANCE.

Or go to: righthouse.com/deep-allegiance

NOTE: flip to the very end to read an exclusive sneak peek...

DON'T MISS ANYTHING!

If you want to stay up to date on all new releases in this series, with this author, or with any of our new deals, you can do so by joining our newsletters below.

In addition, you will immediately gain access to our entire *Right House VIP Library,* which includes many riveting Mystery and Thriller novels for your enjoyment. Including a prequel novella to this series!

righthouse.com/email

(Easy to unsubscribe. No spam. Ever.)

ALSO BY DAVID ARCHER

Up to date books can be found at:
www.righthouse.com/david-archer

ROGUE THRILLERS
Gates of Hell (Book 1)
Hell's Fury (Book 2)
Ice Burn (Book 3)
Judgement by Fire (Book 4)

JACOB HUNTER THRILLERS
The Kyiv File (Book 1)
The Bogota File (Book 2)
The Havana File (Book 3)
The Amsterdam File (Book 4)

PETER BLACK THRILLERS
Burden of the Assassin (Book 1)
The Man Without A Face (Book 2)
Unpunished Deeds (Book 3)
Hunter Killer (Book 4)
Silent Shadows (Book 5)
The Last Run (Book 6)
Dark Corners (Book 7)
Ghost Operative (Book 8)
A Fire Burning (Book 9)
Dawnlight (Book 10)
Dead Ice (Book 11)

ALEX MASON THRILLERS
Odin (Book 1)

Ice Cold Spy (Book 2)
Mason's Law (Book 3)
Assets and Liabilities (Book 4)
Russian Roulette (Book 5)
Executive Order (Book 6)
Dead Man Talking (Book 7)
All The King's Men (Book 8)
Flashpoint (Book 9)
Brotherhood of the Goat (Book 10)
Dead Hot (Book 11)
Blood on Megiddo (Book 12)
Son of Hell (Book 13)
Merchant of Death (Book 14)
Extinction C-14 (Book 15)

NOAH WOLF THRILLERS

Code Name Camelot (Book 1)
Lone Wolf (Book 2)
In Sheep's Clothing (Book 3)
Hit for Hire (Book 4)
The Wolf's Bite (Book 5)
Black Sheep (Book 6)
Balance of Power (Book 7)
Time to Hunt (Book 8)
Red Square (Book 9)
Highest Order (Book 10)
Edge of Anarchy (Book 11)
Unknown Evil (Book 12)
Black Harvest (Book 13)
World Order (Book 14)
Caged Animal (Book 15)
Deep Allegiance (Book 16)
Pack Leader (Book 17)
High Treason (Book 18)
A Wolf Among Men (Book 19)

Rogue Intelligence (Book 20)
Alpha (Book 21)
Rogue Wolf (Book 22)
Shadows of Allegiance (Book 23)
In the Grip of Darkness (Book 24)
Wolves in the Dark (Book 25)
Olympus Must Fall (Book 26)

SAM PRICHARD MYSTERIES
The Grave Man (Book 1)
Death Sung Softly (Book 2)
Love and War (Book 3)
Framed (Book 4)
The Kill List (Book 5)
Drifter: Part One (Book 6)
Drifter: Part Two (Book 7)
Drifter: Part Three (Book 8)
The Last Song (Book 9)
Ghost (Book 10)
Hidden Agenda (Book 11)

SAM AND INDIE MYSTERIES
Aces and Eights (Book 1)
Fact or Fiction (Book 2)
Close to Home (Book 3)
Brave New World (Book 4)
Innocent Conspiracy (Book 5)
Unfinished Business (Book 6)
Live Bait (Book 7)
Alter Ego (Book 8)
More Than It Seems (Book 9)
Moving On (Book 10)
Worst Nightmare (Book 11)
Chasing Ghosts (Book 12)
Serial Superstition (Book 13)

CHANCE REDDICK THRILLERS
Innocent Injustice (Book 1)
Angel of Justice (Book 2)
High Stakes Hunting (Book 3)
Personal Asset (Book 4)

CASSIE MCGRAW MYSTERIES
What Lies Beneath (Book 1)
Can't Fight Fate (Book 2)
One Last Game (Book 3)
Never Really Gone (Book 4)

ABOUT US

Right House is an independent publisher created by authors for readers. We specialize in Action, Thriller, Mystery, and Crime novels.

If you enjoyed this novel, then there is a good chance you will like what else we have to offer! Please stay up to date by using any of the links below.

Join our mailing lists to stay up to date -->
righthouse.com/email
Visit our website --> righthouse.com
Contact us --> contact@righthouse.com

 facebook.com/righthousebooks
 x.com/righthousebooks
 instagram.com/righthousebooks

EXCLUSIVE SNEAK PEEK OF...

DEEP ALLEGIANCE

PROLOGUE

DONALD JEFFERSON WOULD HAVE BEEN THE FIRST TO acknowledge that he didn't spend a lot of time thinking about life. Most of the time, life just rolled by and he went along for the ride. Life is something that changed about as often as you thought about it, anyway. Donald thought it was beautiful, if somewhat frightening at times, and didn't give it a lot more thought than that.

Blatant, subtle, cold, amusing, incidental, sarcastic irony never ceased to entertain life's spectators because it never ceased to surprise them. For Donald Jefferson, the experience never failed to give him pause. He was not a superstitious man, but he was a suspicious one and he believed in irony. He believed in irony the same way some men believe in God, but more than that, he believed in irony the way some believed in paranormal activity, government conspiracies, or alien invasions.

While there were always a dozen or more people ready to stand up and argue the believing man's lack of proof or truth, Donald knew the believers were not altogether wrong. After all, he *was* part of a government conspiracy, the number two man and operations director for the Elimination and Eradication Agency. In that position, he dealt with a number of United States allied governments who occasionally had need of the agency's services and personnel, the acknowledged best in the field of assassination and espionage. E & E was so secret that it never allowed evidence of issued assignments to leave its offices, and occasionally had to leave their own people out in the cold in order to avoid discovery.

Working for E & E had made Donald realize that the religion of irony was a religion of give and take. It gave by putting him in a profession that ran through his blood, a profession he couldn't imagine not doing. It gave him the iron determination to make sure that the men and women he worked with, the men and women he had to send out to kill and infiltrate and destroy the lives of the enemies of America, were the best there could be at what they did.

It took by the way it brought Donald to the knowledge that he was responsible for the lives of people like Noah Wolf and his team, as well as many others. It took by requiring him to trust his own ability to perform his duties in a competent manner, and that trust wasn't something that came to him easily.

Part of those duties involved dealing with the people who were constantly requesting their assistance. In that capacity, Donald occasionally had to travel around the world to meet with diplomatic officials and others who had the authority to request E & E services. It was his job to determine whether those requests were viable enough to pass up the line to his superior, Allison Peterson, the director of the agency.

He constantly calculated every factor involved in each such meeting. This was a habit that was so deeply ingrained in his psyche that he rarely missed even the slightest detail.

It was because of this belief, this honed skill, this ability to read expressions and body language better than almost anyone else, that he'd made the discovery that sent him down another road of intrigue. But it was the *take* part of irony that prevented him from seeing the full picture sooner.

Donald Jefferson was walking into a trap.

Of course, there was no way he could have known that at the

time. His old friend Harold, the Austrian Ambassador to England, had asked him to come and visit for the purpose of arranging a liaison between Chechnya and E & E. The small country had many internal enemies, and some of them were so incorrigible that there was no way to remove them short of assassination, but they were also powerful and well-protected. It would take expertise such as E & E could offer to eradicate them, and Harold had been instrumental in arranging such liaisons in the past. In fact, it was Harold who had convinced the British government to allow the agency to operate in the U.K. when necessary.

Donald and Harold went way back. During the Middle East conflicts, the two of them had been involved in intelligence and had several occasions to work together. Afterward, when Harold went into the diplomatic services, the friendship they had developed became an asset to both of them.

Neither of them knew that Harold was one of many such men whose lives were manipulated and controlled by someone who considered himself the ultimate puppet master.

———

THE WEALTHY AND philanthropic Harold Ingemar's penthouse party was in full swing when Caleb Dawson stepped out of the elevator and smoothly showed his invitation to the doorman.

Inwardly, Dawson scoffed at calling the garish affair a *party*. He hated these things; the pointless yet pointed interactions that only added to the atmosphere of unreasoned privilege, and the arrogant belief of being untouchable. All in attendance were steadfastly ignoring the dirt and grime forty stories below, preferring to believe that the world was as they wished it to be At one time, 'party' had meant casual clothes, loud music, the chance to act like a fool and be loved for it. This expensively catered event drew only those with expensive tastes in everything, people who had their fingers in everything else. These were the kind of people who thought themselves above everyone else, unreachable, even untouchable by the lower and baser parts of the world.

They were really nothing more than idiots. Dawson knew better than anyone that absolutely everyone was touchable.

As he strolled casually but directly across the room to the balcony doors, he tuned out the insignificant conversations and focused on identifying the number of people who were in attendance along with him. Dawson recognized some, but knew none would recognize him. That was how he worked. He didn't often associate with the others. He never stuck around long enough to do so. He never stuck around long enough to even be noticed.

Still in front of the balcony doors, Dawson stopped. Down the stairs to his right was a tall, athletic-looking man in his fifties. This was his target, Donald Jefferson. He was easily identifiable, even without the physical description. Though his serious face fit perfectly with the small group of tuxedoed gentlemen surrounding him, the confident and easy way he stood set him subtly apart.

Dawson held back a grin when he realized the Director himself was among the men Jefferson mingled with. Dawson was rarely given the opportunity to perform his skills right in front of his master.

He would make this interesting, for Spear's sake.

He didn't acknowledge the Director and the Director didn't acknowledge him. Caleb Dawson was the consummate professional, and anonymity was of value to both of them.

Watching Jefferson, Dawson smiled slightly. If all went well, he'd be free from this facade of a party in less than five minutes.

He tucked his invitation smoothly into his pocket and moved onto the balcony. It was empty and he was glad. He pulled a vape pen from his left pocket, its innocent appearance already deadly, loaded with the two centimeter dart that held the drug. From his other pocket, he took the fake battery that held the pressurized CO_2 charge that would launch the tiny dart. He felt an odd sense of pleasure as the pieces locked easily together. He had practice, and it all went together smoothly and soundlessly. There would be no issues.

Fixing the device in his hand, Dawson turned back toward the doors and the elite society to be found behind them, not even glancing at the spectacular London skyline.

When he stepped back into the room, he tracked Jefferson, seeing that he'd moved away from the balcony doors. Casually, Dawson lifted a glass of champagne from a strolling server and watched. Jefferson shifted nearer to the food table, seemingly also seeking a glass of champagne. Dawson sipped carefully. As he lowered the glass from his lips, the drug was fired unceremoniously into Jefferson's neck. His aim was perfect, and no one noticed a thing. Not a ripple of disturbance buzzed the other partygoers.

Jefferson's hand flew to his neck, rubbing at the spot. His eyes were wide, and the "Oh, no," that emerged from his lips was too soft to hear. Dawson couldn't help admiring the instant recognition that shone from his victim's eyes as he searched the room for his killer, realizing instantly what had happened even at a time when most others would have spent their last seconds clinging to denial.

The clarity only lasted a moment, dissipating rapidly as the drug took over.

Dawson's work was done.

Leaving his champagne on the table to his right, he returned to the elevators, ignoring Jefferson clutching his neck less than ten feet away.

The elegant old age-style elevator welcomed him with a friendly ding as he entered calmly and pushed the button to take him back down to the main lobby. He'd traveled only two floors down when he started to hear the screams. By the time he walked out through the building's front doors, a small crowd was gathering around Donald Jefferson's body on the parking lot's hard pavement.

Sirens could already be heard ringing in the distance.

Dawson ignored the first two cab drivers and he was ignored in turn, the drivers too distracted by all the noise and excitement to bother trying to pick up another fare. He slid into the back seat of the third taxi in the line, and the driver didn't even realize he'd picked up a fare for a few seconds.

The job had not taken anywhere near as long as he'd expected, after all, and it was a beautiful night. He'd always enjoyed some of the London night life, and so he decided to go and have a drink. With any luck, one of the girls he'd met the last time he was here would be around.

CHAPTER 1

NOAH WOLF WAS ASLEEP AND DREAMING WHEN THE call came. This one was actually more like a memory, the kind of dream where the sounds and motions of the outside world merge so completely with the images of the mind that the line separating truth and the world of dreams is temporarily wiped away.

In the dream, he was still suffering the effects of his last mission, still afflicted with the emotions that had come flooding back into him as the result of the trauma he had gone through. It was terrifying for Noah to be having those feelings again after so many years, so this dream was as much a nightmare as anything else.

The phone woke him on its very first ring, and for a moment, he thought he was still in the hospital ward. His eyes searched the darkness of his bedroom, looking for any sign that he was still in that reality, but Noah is one of those whose dreams fade away quickly after he wakes.

He blinked and the phone rang again. He snatched it up and put it to his ear, the horror of the dream already forgotten.

"Camelot," he said.

"There is a plane waiting for you at Heathrow," Allison said. "Get your team on board and get here as quickly as you can. As soon as you arrive, Noah, I need to see you. Just you, Noah. Nobody else right now."

There was something in her voice that made asking questions seem like a very bad idea.

"We're on the way," Noah said. "I'll see you tomorrow."

Sarah roused herself as he started to climb out of bed. "Noah? What's going on?"

"Allison wants us back at Neverland," he said. "There's a plane waiting for us at Heathrow, and I'm supposed to see her tomorrow, as soon as we arrive. She said to come to her office alone, so the rest of you will be able to go out to the house and relax." He pulled on his jeans and started toward the door.

Sarah picked up her phone and hit the button to make it light up. "It's only three o'clock in the morning," she said. "What could be so important it couldn't wait until normal hours?"

"I don't know," Noah said, "but I'm going to find out." He stepped out into the hall and woke the others, letting them know that they needed to get up and pack quickly. He made it clear that he didn't know the answer to their questions, so they simply packed up and then headed for the airport.

———

BECAUSE OF THE time difference and the ten hour flight, it was just after seven a.m. when the plane touched down in Kirtland. The van, driven by a new recruit who they didn't recognize, was waiting for them at the airport, and dropped Noah off at the Brigadoon Investments building, the headquarters of E & E. The rest of them stayed in the van and headed out to Noah's house. They would relax there until he came back to tell them what was going on.

Noah rode up in the elevator and walked past the empty receptionist's desk. He opened the door without hesitation to see Allison sitting behind her own desk, and for the first time in many years, Noah found himself slightly surprised when he saw her.

Her face was red, especially around the eyes. Allison Peterson had been crying, and Noah hadn't even believed such a thing would be possible.

"Thank you for coming so quickly," she said. "Sit down, Noah." She tapped on the keyboard of her computer and the screen on the wall behind her snapped to life, showing a collage of photographs: a nondescript brown-haired man engaged in various activities.

Noah instantly memorized the man's face, even before Allison began speaking.

"The first thing I have to tell you is that Donald Jefferson is dead," she said.

Noah's expression did not change as he continued to stare at the photos displayed over her shoulder.

"What happened?" he asked. It was the same way he might ask why the coffee pot was empty.

"He was in London to meet with officials from one of the smaller European countries, to discuss the possibility of E & E helping them with some of their problems. He was attending a private party at the home of the Austrian ambassador that had more security than the President of the United States, and he should have been perfectly safe. Unfortunately, there are a few assassins out there who are almost as good as you. One of them got to Donald in the middle of the reception. He was injected with a drug, something that affected his mind within only a matter of seconds. It caused some sort of terror reaction, because he suddenly appeared frightened of everyone around him and jumped out a fortieth floor window as if he was trying to escape them."

"The killer would be the man on the screen behind you?" Noah asked.

"The man you're looking at is responsible for Donald's death, yes. No one knows his real name. He uses many identities. In this case, he was using the name Caleb Dawson."

"How did you identify him?" Noah asked.

"Security video, of course," Allison replied. "As I said, the affair had terrific security, including hidden video cameras just about everywhere. The footage was handed over to MI6, who shared it with our people over there." She sighed. "From what we have been able to learn, Dawson has for the past couple of years maintained an exclusive contract with a powerful underworld leader whom we know only by the name of Spear."

Spear, Noah thought, surprised that as he rolled the name through his mind, he still felt absolutely nothing. The name should have meant more; hearing the name of Donald's killer should have caused at least a desire to punish the individual, but Noah only considered him a threat that needed to be eliminated. Who in the world was Caleb Dawson, and who was this Spear? What possible motive could they have had for killing Donald?

"Spear," Noah said. "I don't think I've heard the name before. What can you tell me about him?"

"Spear is a manipulator," Allison replied. "All we know about him is that he is known for orchestrating terror events and assassinations that are designed to push governments into doing specific things. To give you an example, he is suspected of being behind the recent mass casualty attacks in Berlin that caused the German government to begin rounding up and deporting Muslim immigrants. That action has led to sanctions against Germany from almost every other nation and has crippled several parts of the German economy. As a result, Germany is now beholden to the rest of the European Union just to continue surviving as a nation."

Noah nodded. "What was Mr. Jefferson doing at the time of his death?"

"Donald was discussing the possibility of opening a liaison office in Chechnya when he was killed. Chechnya has a lot of internal strife, and some of the players are too powerful to touch through conventional means. Harold Ingemar, the Austrian ambassador, was an old friend of Donald's. The Chechnyan government approached him to act as a go-between, and he invited Donald to come and discuss the situation. In order to avoid having Donald go to the Chechnyan Embassy, Ingemar arranged a party at his own home and made sure the ambassador was there. Donald was supposed to speak with him, but never got the chance." She paused for a second, her eyes misty. "We believe the motive for his assassination was to prevent Chechnya from pursuing a relationship with our organization. Their ambassador has declined to continue the discussion."

"Do we have any idea where Dawson is now?"

"No," Allison said. "Sooner or later, however, he will be ordered to kill again and all of our intelligence agencies are scanning for information on when that might take place. I'm sending you and your team, Noah, to find and track this son of a bitch and identify Spear, who is actually responsible for Donald's death. I want you to get started as soon as you can, but not before the day after tomorrow. Donald's body will be arriving back here tomorrow, and his funeral is scheduled for the day after that."

"I'm curious, but why didn't you have his body brought back on the same plane with us?"

"Because there can be no association between you and him. Donald was known as part of our agency; given half a chance, some of our enemies would use the fact that you were on that plane to connect you and your team to the organization, as well. We can't risk that."

"You'll have identity kits and such ready for us by then?"

"Molly is going to be taking over for Donald," Allison said. "She'll be handling such things, so check with her tomorrow. She should have everything ready in plenty of time." She paused and looked at him for a moment. "Noah, Sarah is not going. I'm not risking my grandchild, and don't you dare say a word, by letting her go on this mission."

Noah nodded once, then got to his feet. "I'll take care of it," he said. "Mr. Jefferson was a good man."

A tear snaked its way down Allison's cheek. "He was that," she said. "And a lot more, besides."

Noah recognized the dismissal as he heard it. He got up and walked out of the office, then took the elevator down to the first floor. He wasn't surprised to find Doctor Nathan Parker sitting on the bench outside the front door.

"Doc," Noah said. "Are you waiting for me?"

"Of course," Parker said, getting slowly to his feet. "First, I knew you were going to need a ride out to your house, but there's also the fact that I want to discuss a couple of factors regarding your new mission." He got up off the bench and started toward the Cadillac parked at the curb. "Get in, son, I'm not going to waste a lot of time. We can talk on the way to your place."

Noah followed him and got into the car on the passenger side. Parker slid behind the wheel, started up the car and pulled away from the curb. He didn't say anything until they had passed the first intersection.

"Donald Jefferson was one of the finest men I've ever known. This world is not going to be the place it should be without him in it."

"I can agree with that assessment," Noah said.

"However, we must also remember that Donald was an experienced and capable agent in his own right. He was one of the most powerful men in the free world, being the right hand of the woman who can order the death of any human being for any reason she chooses. I don't believe there is anyone in the world who would not have considered Donald an extension of Allison Peterson, so had he ever suggested that someone needed to die, that suggestion would have been taken as an order by almost any intelligence operative of our country or its allies. Can you understand what I'm saying?"

"Sir, it sounds like you are implying that Donald may have been tempted to use that power from time to time?"

"He was a man, wasn't he? One of the curses about being in my position with this organization is that some of you people seem to think of me as your Father Confessor. Donald was one who made a point of catching up with me from time to time, so

I'm privy to a few things that even Allison may not know. While our intelligence does indicate that Spear is behind the assassination, I need you to be aware that there could be other factors involved. Some of those factors could exist within our own government."

"Mr. Jefferson had enemies, then," Noah said. "Do you have any reason to believe one of those was responsible for the assassination?"

"I don't even have a reason to believe the sun will come up tomorrow morning," Parker said, "not at my age. There is absolutely nothing certain in this world, Noah, other than the truth you see directly in front of your eyes at a given moment. Truth has a habit of mutating itself; it is always possible that, no matter what the evidence in front of you might suggest, there can be another explanation for any event you can imagine. All I'm trying to say to you is that, while I expect you to carry out your mission and eliminate Spear, you need to be aware that there could be other forces at work, as well."

"Very well, sir," Noah said. "I'll make a note of it and pay close attention to what's happening around us."

"You do that, Noah," Parker said. "And I want you to do yourself one more favor. My gut says you're going to need somebody on this mission who isn't on any intelligence radar. It needs to be somebody who can mold himself to whatever situation comes along. I know that you have absolute autonomy on planning your missions, but I'm going to make a suggestion and I hope you'll take it to heart."

"Please go ahead, sir," Noah said. "A suggestion from you is always going to be welcome."

Parker glanced over at him, then cut his eyes back to the road. "Gary Mitchell," he said. "Gary is the acting coach, I'm sure you remember him. He helped you prepare for a couple of missions in the past, I believe. Gary is a chameleon; he can be whoever he needs to be, even down to making incredibly complex alterations to his appearance. Take him along, and do your best to bring him back. He's a valuable asset in his regular job with us, but I think he may be even more valuable to you in this particular case."

"I'm sure it's going to be an infiltration mission," Noah said. "I think he may be quite valuable indeed."

They chatted about mundane things for the rest of the ride, and then Parker dropped Noah off at his country home. Noah walked in the house and found that everyone had gone back to sleep when they arrived, so he stripped down quickly and crawled into bed beside Sarah.

He was awakened a few hours later by the sound of Neil coming into the house from his trailer across the yard. As he sat up to begin getting dressed, Sarah rolled over and looked at him.

"I didn't even hear you come in," she said. "I never seem to be able to get any rest when I sleep on airplanes. I was so tired when we got here that I just flopped in the bed and was asleep in no time."

"That's all right," Noah said. "We should all take every opportunity to rest, especially with a mission hanging over our heads."

Sarah let out a sigh. "There's a mission, then? What is it this time?"

"Come on out into the living room," Noah said. "I need to tell everyone at the same time." He pulled on his jeans and tugged a T-shirt over his head, then walked out of the room in his bare feet. Sarah got up quickly and dressed herself, then followed and found them all in the kitchen, rather than the living room. Renée had made coffee, and they were all sitting around the table. Sarah got a cup for herself and sat down with them.

"All right," Neil said, "she's here. What's all this about? Why did we have to come back over here so soon?"

"Donald Jefferson is dead," Noah said. "He was assassinated in London the night before last. The assassin has been identified, and Allison believes she knows who was behind it. We are going to eliminate both of them."

There was silence at the table for several seconds, and then all of them tried to speak at once. At first, they all tried to deny what

Noah had said, but his calm demeanor told them he was telling the truth. When they finally came to the point of acceptance, each of them had something to say about Jefferson, and Noah simply let them talk until they were finished.

"We'll be meeting with Molly tomorrow, she'll be taking over Mr. Jefferson's duties. She'll have our identity kits and such ready for us by then." He looked at his wife. "You will be sitting this one out. I'm not taking you out on any more missions. Marco can drive, and so can I. In fact, we all can."

"Neil can't," Marco said, and Neil shot him a glare.

Sarah stared at Noah for a second, and then her face clouded up. "Now, you just wait a…"

"Allison agrees with me," Noah said. "I think you may be the precedent for a new rule, which will probably state that pregnant operatives do not go into the field."

Sarah sputtered, but gave up on arguing. "I'm not going to be happy about this," she said. "Remember what happened the last time you went out on a mission without me."

"That time he went without all of us," Neil said. "Don't worry, Sarah, we will take care of him."

"Of course we will," Jenny said. "We all have his back, Sarah."

A sigh escaped her as Sarah settled back into her chair. "I know you do," she said. "And I understand why I can't go, because of the baby. I just hate the idea of us being apart."

Noah took her hand and smiled at her. "I understand, babe."

———

THE FOLLOWING MORNING, Noah walked into Allison's office again, this time followed by Neil, Jenny, Marco and Renée. Molly was there waiting for them, looking slightly uncomfortable as she sat at the same spot Donald Jefferson had always occupied.

"The nature of this mission is different from many of your other missions in the past," Molly began. "You are to locate and engage Caleb Dawson, then maintain some form of surveillance on him until he leads you to Spear. At that point, your orders are to eliminate both of them. How you achieve the mission, of course, is entirely up to you, Noah, but I have your mission identities ready."

She picked up a large fabric shopping bag and reached inside it, producing a wallet, a watch and a cell phone in a plastic bag. "Noah, your identity for this mission is William Rogers. Your back story is that of a purchasing representative for a large tobacco company." She handed the bag over to him, and he began looking at the photos and other items inside the wallet. Most of them were mundane, probably even nonsensical, but they would lend credibility to the identity, should they be examined by police or other agencies.

Molly withdrew another bag and passed it to Neil. "Neil, you are Leonard Roth, CEO of Roth Technologies. The company produces security software for computers, and actually does exist. It's one of the front companies for E & E, so it was easy to insert you as its CEO."

She took a purse out of the bag and handed it to Jenny. "Jenny, your name is Jennifer Roth, and you are Leonard's wife. Your back story indicates that you were his high school sweetheart and that you are responsible for marketing for the company. Again, should anyone bother to check, both the website and the company staff will confirm your position."

Another purse went to Renée. "Renée, you are Abigail Willis. Your back story is that you are an effective executive assistant, working regularly for temporary agencies throughout the world. One of the jobs you held was actually for Roth Technologies, while they were expanding into Europe."

The final reach into the bag produced another plastic bag filled with wallet, cell phone, etc. "Marco, you are Jeremiah Duchesne. This takes advantage of your Cajun upbringing, so you can let your accent out again. Your back story makes you a former government agent from the United States, now occasionally involved in some shady deals. That identity might come in handy on this mission, and we have built an extensive record of various nefarious activities. You will find a list of them in the cell phone, so you need to scan through it and memorize as many as possible."

Each of them took a moment to examine what they had been given, and then Noah looked at Molly.

"What about Gary Mitchell?" he asked. "I had put in a request to have him assigned to the team for this mission."

"And it's been approved," Allison said. "He's being advised of that fact this morning, and will be waiting for you at R&D. He'll already have his identity kit."

"Which I'm basing on his real past," Molly said. "If he's checked out by the authorities, he will come up as an actor who is looking for work."

Noah nodded. "All right, then. How soon do we leave?"

"As soon as we get any information on where you can find Dawson," Allison said, and then she licked her lips. "Noah, we're having Donald's funeral in the morning, and I thought you would all want to be there."

"Of course we do," Noah said, and the rest nodded their agreement.

Scan the QR code below to purchase DEEP ALLEGIANCE.
Or go to: righthouse.com/deep-allegiance

www.ingramcontent.com/pod-product-compliance
Lightning Source LLC
Chambersburg PA
CBHW020406210626
46816CB00006BB/2142